I0567260

What's a Poor Girl To Do

Fred Andersen

Palavr Publ
ARIZONA, U.S.A.

What's a Poor Girl to Do © 2021 by Fred Andersen
Print Edition

All rights reserved. No part of this book may be reproduced or transmitted in any form by any means, electronic or mechanical, including photocopying, recording, or by any information storage and retrieval system, without permission in writing from the publisher.

Names, characters, businesses, places, events, locales, and incidents are either the products of the author's imagination or used in a fictitious manner. Any resemblance to actual persons, living or dead, or actual events is coincidental.

Palavr Publ/Phoenix, Arizona
palavrpubl@gmail.com
Cover art © 2021 by Fred Andersen
Second Edition February 2021

ISBN: 978-1-7368454-1-7

For C.
We could.

CHAPTER ONE
Summer, 1944

Priscilla

PRISCILLA WAS STILL lying in bed when the phone rang that morning. She had done two performances the previous day in *Hold on to Your Hats*, a silly musical that required a lot of energy from the second female lead, twenty-year-old Priscilla Tash. Showbiz was tough, even in South Dakota. But since today was Monday she would have a well-deserved day off. As a child in a theatre family she took certain things for granted.

The phone had stopped ringing, and she thought she might drift off for a while longer. But there was a knock on the bedroom door and her father's voice. "Priscilla, call for you. Long-distance. Collect."

She threw back the bedsheet and padded barefoot down to the phone in the entry hall. It had to be Ken, to tell her about the new show, which was sure to be exciting. His success, the next step into their future.

But it was not Ken.

"Priscilla? This's Joe."

At first she didn't understand. "Joe?"

"Yeah, Joe Gianelli, Ken's—"

"Yes, Joe!" She remembered him now. Ken's friend. "Has something happened?"

"Something has definitely happened." He chuckled roughly. "I'm here in Lansdale, P.A. And your sweetheart

Kenny is in jail."

"*What?*" Priscilla felt like she'd been slapped. "What do you mean?"

"Well, he got himself into some trouble and he phoned me to come bail him out. So here I am, standing in a phone booth in a coffee shop across the street from the sheriff's office."

This was dizzying. "But he's doing the show, in New York."

"No, he got canned. They changed the role from a college kid to a comic fatso."

"Oh, no!" She felt hope draining away. "But what's that to do with Pennsylvania? Is he alright?"

"He's not hurt." Joe let out a big breath, and Priscilla's anxiety increased. "Well, when he lost the job, he kind of lost his mind. He says, he's *through,* and leavin' New York and he's gonna go work in a logging camp somewhere or something, so stupid. And he was hitchhiking out there to where you're at and gonna break it to you."

"A logging camp?" Priscilla was incredulous. Ken had a bad back. That's how he'd got out of the army. "He couldn't."

"Of course not. But he sorta went off his nut. So anyway, he takes off, and the next thing I know I get a call at one in the morning, and he's in jail here. The story he told me was that a woman picked him up, and she had a bottle, and they got soused, and then he was driving, and cracked up the car. So he's in jail."

Priscilla, not sure she could trust her legs any longer, eased down onto the straight-back chair next to the phone table. She knew her father was around the corner in the parlor, listening. She could almost see the dark, dismissive look that would be on his face.

She'd met Kenny Preston right after starting at the New York Academy of Dramatic Arts the previous fall. Ken was easily the most charismatic male in the academy. Girls there outnumbered boys 2.25 to one, Priscilla once figured out on a dull evening. Most of the scenes the students worked on were man-woman, so the boys were always in demand, and almost all of them let that go to their head. Not Ken. He wasn't tall or especially good looking, but he had an impressive bearing, a reserve that was either great strength or great vulnerability. He watched her once doing a bit from *The Barretts of Wimpole Street* in the rehearsal room, and as she walked out he fell in beside her.

"Are you a classically trained, you know, actress?"

His attempt at sophistication made her laugh. "You don't know where I'm from."

"Yes, I actually do. You're Priscilla, from Sioux City."

Priscilla was impressed, but she wouldn't show it. "Sioux Falls. Sioux City's a burg."

"Really? Should I know that?"

"Absolutely. Where are you from?"

"Denton, Texas. Not Ponder. Ponder's a burg."

She laughed again and that's how it started. He had been in productions since junior high. So those were two things they could talk about, the sticks and the boards. He had a lot of talent, but there was also a hidden part of him, something that held him back, a secret side that she set about trying to uncover. In a week he was walking her to dinner and then back to her hotel every night. In a month it was quite clear that he had marriage on his mind. But Priscilla still wasn't sure enough about him.

Then the school year had ended and she'd gone back to work in summer stock at her parents' small theater. This was something she'd done since childhood, but in 1942 the season had been cancelled because of the war, and in 1943 it had been shortened. This year there was a feeling in the air that the fighting was almost over, so their theater was putting on ten weeks of shows. She was excited about it and her father had offered Kenny a job. But he'd decided to stay in New York, looking for work. And found a great opportunity.

But now . . . She spoke into the pbone. "I don't know what to say. But you have talked to him?"

"Yeah, I just left the jail. The bail bond is fifty dollars. And to tell you the truth, I'm not inclined to try to do that for him. To tell you the truth, I'm a little disgusted with him."

"Oh, Joe, but you have to!" Priscilla did some quick calculating. "If it's a matter of money, I can repay—"

"They only take cash. Pretty much I would have to go back to New York to get it."

"And where are you?"

"Lansdale, about forty miles north of Philly."

"Just a minute, Joe. Hang on." Priscilla set the receiver on the table and steeled herself. Her father had been a little miffed when Ken turned down the job. And he was more or less disdainful of all his daughters' suitors.

When she stepped around the corner, her father was sitting there watching her.

"Daddy, I need to borrow fifty dollars."

"No."

"Please, Daddy, I'll pay you back."

He stood up, walked over to the fireplace, and leaned against the hearth on two stiff arms. "We've never even met this guy. Never even talked to."

Priscilla had to win. "Please, Daddy, I'll pay you—"

"No." He turned and stood facing her. "No. I want *him* to pay me back."

"Thank you, Daddy." Priscilla didn't smile. She knew how angry he was. She went back and picked up the phone and found out from Joe where exactly to wire the money.

When the call was over, she sat by the phone thinking of nothing, and everything. It was so hard to know what to do. Ken was the first *man* she had loved, and she was no longer a girl. Love between grown-up people was both deeper and more complicated than anything she'd experienced. She sometimes felt a desperate longing for him, and he could be so thoughtful and sweet. But things would set him off, or turn him away from her, and then she never knew what to do. He wouldn't accept help or advice. So all she could do was just listen, let him blow off steam. And hope he'd regain his balance.

She heard a step on the front porch and a little squeak, which she recognized as the mailbox being opened. She rose and opened the front door and stepped out onto the porch. There was a letter from Ken.

"Hi darling,

Not much doing here. Hope your life is not so boring. I'm headed down to rehearsal soon. This job is going to be perfect for me, I can just tell . . ."

Knowing what it had meant to him and how crushing the rejection would be, made her heart sink. Maybe he'd been fired an hour after mailing this letter. Maybe that was how quickly it had turned bad for him. And her here, out of reach, not even knowing he was in trouble. She had asked Joe to have Ken call her, and hoped that would happen pretty soon. She wished she had told him to call no matter what, since she had no idea how to get ahold of them. All she could do was wait.

It was a sunny, quiet morning. A milk truck was making its way slowly toward downtown, and the Pascoe boy across the street was pushing a lawn mower along in front of his house. Priscilla picked up the newspaper that was sitting on the chair and sat down. The headline said that the Germans had surrendered Paris. That was joyful news, but she folded the paper and lay it on her lap, wondering what was going on with Ken.

Anna

IT WAS JUST a train trip, but it felt like they had escaped from hell. Berlin was about ready to collapse from the bombing which came day and night, the soldiers' deaths, and lack of everything needed for life. You couldn't find a doctor if you wanted one, or an electrician. You could not find a hairdresser, but here was one sitting right next to Anna. The cast and crew were headed to Salzburg, which had been largely untouched by war. They were going there to make a movie, because the Propaganda Ministry wanted to make sure that the poor suffering people of Berlin could still go to the movies a couple of times a week.

But then the train stopped. "There's planes coming," said someone. Amalia, the hairdresser, looked at Anna with squinting, worried eyes. "They love to bomb the trains," said someone else. None of this needed to be spoken, and Anna felt a little impatient with people saying and re-saying the obvious. But they still did it, and one man said something Anna did not know, that when there was an air raid, trains would try to stop in the woods if possible, to hide from the planes. And they happened to be in a forested area when the train stopped. "So we're lucky," said the man.

"But they might not come at all." Anna patted her friend on the knee. She could feel that hope in the quiet breathing of the people around her. The passengers stood or sat—the train had been very crowded the whole way—staring out the windows at the trees, the sun shining on the weeds along the track.

Most of the windows had lost their glass, which meant a lot of smoke and wind when the train was moving, but now nothing came in but the sunshine and a few horseflies. Anna was staring absently out the window toward the rear of the train, which followed the tracks in a slight curve to her left. Suddenly there was a flash of something on the ground near the track, and another flash, closer, and another, fast, like lightning, and the pop of each missile as it hit. Everyone around Anna gasped or cried out. There was no time to do anything else. Then they could hear the screaming of the planes, and the pops were coming from the other direction, toward the front of the train.

"To hell with this," yelled one man, jumping through the window and landing on the ground with an *oof*. He clambered to his feet and scuttled into the trees. But just as suddenly, it was quiet. Where the rockets had landed, little fires burned in the weeds and trash. The passengers now were all leaving the train as quickly as they could. After all, if the planes came once, they could come again.

"They're Americans," said Mathew, who was only about fourteen. "You can tell by the sound." He pointed up. He was a student, like Anna and Amalia, who had all become unpaid workers at the state film studio, where they filled whatever helpful role they could. That was why they were on this train. Anna made her way to the end of the car and down, holding onto Amalia's hand, and they crawled under the car as best they could, trying to save their knees and skirts from the dirt and cinders, under the car, near the wheels. No sooner had they settled to ground than the rockets came again, up near the engine, and bullets buzzed through the trees like loud, terrible hornets, snapping branches and ripping leaves. Then a shattering, screeching sound and an explosion. Burning debris firing out in all directions. "They got the locomotive," someone said, unnecessarily.

Amalia whispered to Anna, "We are in hell."

Anna Andrzejewski had grown up in a drab neighborhood near the Mottlau river in the Danzig Free State, a Polish and German goulash of a city on the coast of the Baltic

Sea. She was old enough to be frightened by the German invasion of 1939, though most of her schoolmates and her parents' friends said it was a good thing. But soon her Polish neighbors were being sent off to work camps. She escaped their fate because she was of mixed German and Kashubian ancestry and spoke German, and, she knew, because she was tall and blonde and pretty. Her father was too old to be conscripted into the army when the war started, and was able to get a job as an agent on the German national railway, eventually transferring to Berlin and bringing his family. This was where Anna attended her last year of secondary school. She was then accepted as an apprentice in the art department of UFA, the big film studio. Anna's great desire was to be an actress and singer, and she appeared in a few crowd scenes—and then helped the crew move the scenery. In truth, by then, everyone was part of the crew.

Now she was hiding under a train somewhere south of Nürnberg, in the gravest possible danger. At least, Anna reflected, since the engine was blown up, the train would not move, and so she would not be crushed under the heavy steel wheels next to her.

But then it was over. The planes were gone, the fires seemed to be dying down in the damp earth and foliage of the forest, and the passengers around her let go of their fear and began to move around. With the locomotive gone, it would be a long wait. Something would be done, eventually, but what or when it would be was beyond guessing. Had anyone been hurt? Who was in charge now? Would they walk to a town? Get a new locomotive? Were the tracks alright? A lazy buzz of rumors circulated up and down the length of the train. So they waited. What else could they do?

A conductor came by, passing out food from the train. Anna reached toward him and received a ham roll. She tore it with her fingers and gave half to Amalia.

Mrs. Brown

CARLA BROWN LOVED her relaxing cup of tea in the evening, especially on a wet, blustery night like this, with the first storm of the fall blowing in. Nineteen forty-four had been a good year for her, the best since Steve died. Her son Greg was growing up, and at the age of seven, becoming a real person, someone she could actually talk to, at times. And getting easier to care for.

That in turn meant she had more time for a social life, which for her meant her girlfriends and people from church. Men weren't interested in a widow with a young son, especially one with problems. She loathed that look people would get when Greggy did something unexpected, that closed off look that said, *I don't want to know!*

And best of all, her job was going fabulously. As executive assistant to Morton Blackwell she was in a position of real importance and real rewards. She dealt with contracts and talent, with finance, with scheduling and distribution and even advertising. Everything but the creative supervision of the movies themselves, which remained Mort's department. And his obsession.

She made enough now to afford the little house across the street from the park, just a half-mile from the studio. And she could get the best help: Greggy's school, and Mrs. Plambeck, their housekeeper and nanny.

A gust of breeze rattled the window of the kitchen alcove where she sat with Greggy while he finished his cookies and tea.

"Boop boop ditum datum whatum choo," sang Greggy. It was the song about the three little fishies. "And they swam and they swam all over that dam. Now you sing, Mommy, you sing the first part."

"Down in the meadow in a little bitty pool," she sang. "Swam three little fishies and a mama fishy too."

Routine was so important for him. And for her, too. Home by six thirty, dinner at seven, take a bath or play until eight thirty, then his little snack and cup of herbal tea, then tuck into bed, and he would drop off, safe and sound.

It was a good life—the result of hard work, good decisions and just doing what you have to do. Things had never been better.

✧ ✧ ✧

She had just put Greggy down when the phone rang. She picked it up. "Hello?"

There was a sound like wind, or the phone rubbing on cloth, and a distant, garbled voice.

Carla repeated, "Hello?"

"Miz B! Gotta help me!"

She thought she recognized the voice, but the words were so strange. "Who is—"

"It's Mort. I need help. I'm . . . office. Right away, if you can, *oh, please.* Don't call police. Don't call 'em! Please come down."

She stood rooted for a few seconds, uncertain what to say or do. It really sounded like Morton Blackwell, but it didn't at all. And the request was so—

"Carla, can you hear me?" Now it sounded much more like her boss. "I need help, right away. I'm at the office. I need you to come down right away. But don't say anything to anybody, okay?"

"Yes, okay! I'm on the way!"

"Use the private entrance."

"Okay, I will." Carla fought off the urge to ask what

happened. She would find out soon enough.

"And don't call the police!" rasped the voice.

✧   ✧   ✧

THE FIRST THING she had to do was cut off the electrical cords.

The private door in back was standing open when she arrived. Whatever had happened, Mort obviously did not want the security men at the front of the building to know about it. When she walked in, she knew why. The lamp lay tossed into the middle of the floor. Mort leaned on his desk looking anxious and disheveled. The cord from the lamp had been pulled out and tied around his wrists. Shoelaces had been used on his ankles.

In his struggles to get free he had only pulled the knots tighter, so they were like little iron nuts. Mrs. Brown got the big pair of scissors out of her desk and wedged them between his skin and the wire. It required some effort and pulling before the scissors bit all the way through, and she worried about cutting or scraping him. He already looked pretty beat up. And he smelled like alcohol and . . . some bodily function.

When he was free, the first thing she asked was, "How did you manage to dial the phone?"

Mort, rubbing his wrists, briefly showed her how he'd twisted his bound arms around from his back until he could see his fingers, and stick one in the dialer.

"They got it all," Mort growled. "I'm such a dumb fuck. Such a dumb fuck!" He spat out the words. Carla glanced at the wall safe. The Modigliani on hinges that was supposed to cover the safe was swung open. The safe was also open.

Carla felt a little surge of exasperation. "Who was it?"

He slumped down into the swivel chair behind the desk. "Ge' me some water, willya?"

She went to the little wet bar recessed into the wall and ran a cup of water out of the tap. As he drank, she asked again, "Who—"

"The game was a setup."

"This was your poker game?"

"It was craps. They wouldn't take my marker, or a check. It was a setup. It was Brooks."

"Who's Brooks?"

"It's the guy I owe a buncha money to." He moved his jaw around with his hand.

"How much did you lose?"

"Two thou. They made me come back here to get it. When we got here they pulled out guns and made me open the safe. So they got ten grand, and they let me know this was for Brooks, and they tied me up and kicked the shit out of me. Then they said, we're gonna get a bag big enough to hold your body, and we'll come back. I think they broke a rib." He took a deep sobbing breath and winced. "They beat me *after* I gave them the money." Tears squeezed out of his eyes.

She knew he had a shadow life—the gambling, the booze. Or better to say, she knew as much as she wanted to know. There had always been telephone calls, and visitors, and errands that she knew were not about business, but about some trouble he'd gotten into, or shady character he'd met. "You've got to go to the hospital."

"No, I'm alright. I'll be alright."

She thought about Mort's wife. "I should call Elaine."

"No. No need for that. She couldn't do anything more than what you're doing."

Carla was wadding the bits of electrical cord into a ball. "You mean, cutting off the ropes from the . . . How much do you owe this guy?"

"Fifty grand."

"Good lord!" cried Carla. She couldn't even grasp how

that was possible. This was one of the most powerful men in Hollywood. He made and broke people with a wave of a pen. Yet here he was, whimpering, helpless. "And they took how much tonight, along with the pound of flesh?"

"Ten."

She dropped the ball of cords into the wastebasket. "You, my friend, need to find a new hobby."

CHAPTER TWO

January 1947

Lyman Wilbur

HE HAD PULLED out his old worsted suit the day before, tried it on, thought about it, then went to May Co. and bought something off the rack. They did the alterations right there— with Lyman that always meant taking up the sleeves. This morning he woke up, made a pot of coffee, sat and thought for a while, then got up, shaved, combed his hair, polished his shoes, moving deliberately, savoring and thinking about each action as if he would never do this thing again. Finally he put on the new suit, checked the mirror and checked pockets for his wallet and keys. He had plenty of time and walked slowly through the house, which had been put in spotless order by the maid, with everything placed where it should be. Where she would look for it.

He heard the car in the driveway and went to the front door, turning for one last survey of the living room that she had designed, the furniture and paintings and frames and lamps she had decided on, the Italianate touches, the golds and greens, the shiny, painted ceramic bowls and vases, the dark wood arms and legs of the chairs curved and carved in floral designs.

They met after the First World War, while Tina was still married to Augustus DiMarche, an artist and bon vivant of a still earlier era. She was a beauty, a free spirit, a bohemian with money. Lyman was attracted to her immediately but didn't consider an affair, refusing not on moral grounds, but in deference to his opinion of himself as being above that sort of tawdriness. What an insufferable prig he had been then. And yet . . .

He heard the car door slam and went out, shutting the heavy door of their home behind him with the solid thud it always took.

Newman was halfway up the walk. "Hi," he said. He took Lyman's hand and gave him a soft clap on the shoulder. "How you doin'?"

"Fine, fine. You know."

"Good." Newman was undoubtedly Lyman's oldest real friend, now sagging and mottled with age, but sturdy as an oak in his sympathetic understanding. "You ready for this?"

"Yes, I guess I have to be." They went to the car. The dewy morning had turned into a bright, cloudless, breezy winter day, the sun cool and low in the sky. Lyman got in on the passenger side of the car. "Thanks again—"

"Of course. Do you, ah—" Newman slid a silver flask out of his jacket.

Lyman shook his head. "I'm doing this without a net."

"Sure." Newman pocketed the flask and started the car. As they drove, Newman spoke of a dinner some years before. "It was the Ambassador Hotel, wasn't it? She was like the queen that night. everyone who walked in knew her. Bankers, lawyers, city councilmen. I can't remember all their names, but Tina sure could."

"Well, yeah. That was an extraordinary night. I remember it. Yes. But that went back to her early years, with Augie. She was a force in this town, socially, with the business and cultured set. You weren't around then, the early twenties."

"No."

"She was something."

"I'll bet she was."

Newman steered the car downtown. Rosewood was

where the old money types hung around. She would be comfortable there, in the ground next to her first husband, who had been waiting almost twenty-five years. There would be no church service, just a few words by a jack-of-all minister, or maybe not even a minister, just a serious man in a conservative suit. Lyman had let the funeral director handle all that. His job today would be to represent Tina, and her choice to marry him, and it was very important to him to do that with all the dignity and humanity the occasion deserved. Because the choice to marry Lyman had taken her away from the exciting, energetic life she had known before.

Newman somehow knew exactly where to go, and they pulled up to a pretty big crowd of people. Lyman moved through the faces, those artists and poets of the past.

In the early twenties—how quaint that sounded now, in this freighted age—before movies entirely took over everything, Los Angeles had a literary, artistic *monde*. Poets, painters, architects, littérateurs. And Tina and Augustus—Augie—were patrons of that world when patronage of real artists amounted to serving dinner and plenty of wine.

Lyman himself was a dilettante then, a low-level player in industrial real estate, with aspirations to poetry. He applied himself to work, and when Augustus died of an infection in 1924, he proposed to Tina almost immediately. Lyman by then had some confidence in his own future, and he feared she would get other offers. She accepted, but they waited two years to get married, two years in which, as they used to say, his prospects increased. She was older than he, and not by just a couple of years. It didn't matter.

He moved across the sparse lawn toward the grave. Everyone looked at him, some more directly than others. Lyman's own friends, mostly writers from his magazine days, stood at the back of the crowd. Lyman would shake their hands later and accept their regrets, which would be sincere and awkward. He didn't know many people from the studio, but Fred Sheldrake and April Sheffield were here. Sheldrake hiring him to work at Colosseum Pictures had allowed Lyman to give Tina at least a few years of comfort and security at the end.

But most of these people had not been part of his or Tina's life for twenty-odd years. He was already a drunk when he courted and married her, though no one said that to him because he was a successful drunk, floating along on a sun-dappled river of booze and self-regard. But then his success went away and the whiskey and gin dumped into a sewer. By the time he dried up they had lost almost everything, including most of her old crowd. Lyman regretted this, of course, but in later years he came to believe that this time of struggle had made them, had strengthened their love, and the character of both of them. Really, it was the best time of their life. And that was mostly because of what, or who, Tina turned out to be. He was writing stories for the pulp mags, barely getting the bills paid. But her quiet strength, humor, and wisdom demanded more of Lyman, and he learned how to give it.

For all those reasons and thoughts and questions Lyman went dry through the service and the condolences. Since there was no reception planned, people stood around for a half an hour or more on the grass afterwards, chatting, remembering, reacquainting. In the end he sent Newman home and stood alone at the gravesite, in a lovely breeze coming off the sea. He said his goodbye—yes, his long goodbye—feeling the thrum of spirit and attachment and love and loss like a deep and long-held bass note on some cosmic viola. And then he turned and walked away. And he told himself he would never come back. He went to the cemetery office where they called him a cab, and was taken to a hotel where he checked in, because he could not stand to go back to the home they had shared.

And he brought a bottle. Actually, four.

Morton Blackwell . . .

SAT IN HIS usual booth at his favorite restaurant in downtown Los Angeles. The Windsor was an enclosed island of red leather upholstery populated by obsequious waiters in bow ties and slicked back hair. Business was done here.

He turned to his third-favorite director. "Well?"

Koehler pursed his lips a little and nodded. His sour headmaster look. "Potential is there."

They both looked with frank appraisal at Priscilla, the young actress Mort had brought from New York. "Yes," said Mort. "There's something. With very natural makeup she could play a teenager. And a saint."

"She may *be* a saint." Koehler chuckled. "You beatified, Mrs. Preston?"

"Hardly." Priscilla Preston did not smile. "Hardly. I grew up in theatre."

"Then I am astounded," said Koehler. "No dissipation. No cynicism."

Mort ignored the witticisms. "Yes, there's something fresh there."

Priscilla blushed and gave them an uncertain smile. She obviously had not meant the comment to be smart or sarcastic. Thus proving Koehler's point.

Mort was hoping Koehler would agree to direct his new picture, *Angeline.* But Henry was a free agent, so he would only do it if he believed in the project. And believing in this project required believing in the character at the center of it and the actress who would portray her.

There were a lot of pieces to that. Mort had talked to, tested, and auditioned three dozen actresses, and rejected applications and calls by dozens of others or their agents. All this interest was fueled by the popularity of the book to which Mort held the rights, the romanticized biography of St. Angeline, a fifteenth-century noblewoman who ended up a nun. Everyone recognized that Angeline could be a star-making role. But there was more to consider than just the actress's ability. There was also image to think about. You couldn't pass off a slattern as a saint. Did the public know her already, and if so, in what roles? Did they have a preconceived notion of the actress based on publicity, background, or even just her looks? Mort's dissatisfaction with everyone he had seen had led him to launch a wider search. He wanted a new face, but that face had to be attached to sturdy shoulders that could carry a picture. That's a tough combination to find.

He had finally found this girl in the cast of a humdrum New York play. She had a look: medium height, slender, with deep, dark-brown eyes and dark-brown hair and the sort of facial construction that a movie camera loves. That natural, unforced innocence she projected couldn't be true, yet somehow it was. And somewhere inside there was a fire of wisdom or passion or ambition or, well, just something. That's what Mort saw. The thing that the great ones have that shines through even in corny dialogue, in badly shot scenes, in the most predictable plots. But when given the right role in the right movie, the real stars light up the screen.

Having found her, Morton Blackwell was going all in on this girl. He better be right. *She* better be right. But Mort had confidence. Part of being a gambler is believing in your bets. While the others at the table thought about the girl, Mort dived into his Crab Louie. But he did want to make one point. "If we pick her, we'll sort of be hiding her light under a . . . what do they hide it under, Albie?"

"Under a bushel," Albie the publicity man jumped in, veteran wordsmith that he was. "A bushel basket. But they leave off the basket."

"Right. At least until we come up with your new name.

Then we'll start leaking stuff out." Mort wanted to reassure Priscilla. "But don't worry, that's just temporary, to help build the picture. After it comes out everyone will know you. And then we'll do something totally opposite, so you'll have a chance to show your range. You can be a gorgeous hussy."

"That would be wonderful!" said Priscilla.

Henry chuckled. Mort had a good feeling about him, though not yet a firm commitment. Mort would let him think about it over the weekend. If he couldn't get Koehler he would use one of his staff men, probably Vincent. But he was used to getting what he wanted, and had a strong feeling that Koehler would be on board by Monday. And the planned start of filming in three weeks would go smoothly.

He drove her back to the hotel in Culver City. It was a fine but not fashionable inn, away from Hollywood-Beverly Hills snoopers and temptations, and just a few blocks from the studio. His studio. Blackwell Pictures. Two Best Pictures in its first five years.

Priscilla had been charmed by the hotel, of course, since she'd been living in a dumpy row house in Brooklyn with her husband, just scraping by. This hotel represented hope for the future, and a plan to get there.

As they approached the hotel, he said, "Well, we've still got a lot to talk about. Preproduction is rolling along now. So tomorrow—"

"Say, can we talk about it now?"

"Sure, but, you're not tired?"

"Oh no!" Priscilla flashed a smile. "Why don't you come up?"

As they rode up in the smooth, quiet elevator, she said. "I've been so excited about all the preparations. And I won't let you down."

"I'm sure you won't."

Priscilla continued to chatter brightly as they walked to her room. She turned on a lamp, took off her coat and hung it over the back of a chair. She had not worn a hat, per

Mort's instructions, and her makeup had been done under his direction, all for the purpose of giving Koehler sort of preview of her as Angeline. Of course she couldn't wear period costume, since the period was the 1400s, but the face was what Mort wanted to sell.

She walked over to the window and looked out at the darkness. "I don't want to let you down. I'll do my best, but . . ." She turned and walked back toward him. "I know I can do it, but I'm still afraid. It's hard to understand." She stopped in front of him and ran a finger under the lapel of his coat as if studying the material.

Mort was taken pleasantly by surprise. She wasn't obviously pushy or brazen, but here she was standing right in front of him, asking to be embraced. "It's natural to be nervous," he said, consciously maintaining a normal tone of voice. "Who wouldn't be? But we're going to do this right. Henry puts up a sort of crusty front, but he is a superb director."

"I'm sure he's great," she murmured.

"You'll love it at our studio." He reached into his coat pocket for the cigarette case, creating a little space. "We're a family, not a factory. Everyone will try to help you. And whatever help you need, ask Mrs. Brown. She'll be your best friend.".

"She's already helped me so much." Mort offered her a cigarette and lit them with his Ronson. Priscilla walked back to the window, took a drag of the cigarette, then set it in an ashtray. She turned and paced back toward him, staring down at her clasped hands, as if summoning courage. For just a moment Mort wondered if the anxiety he was seeing indicated the soul of an artist or the thrashing of someone doomed to fail.

Now she stood before him again and looked up into his eyes, and Mort suddenly knew—. She *is* the one! This *will* work! I've done it! This is the success I've been waiting for, the return of Mort Blackwell, the beginning of a legendary run of the best and most popular movies ever made! He embraced her, and when her lips brushed his expectantly he kissed her hard, and she responded with a fire that made his heart leap up into this throat.

"Oh, Mr. Blackwell," she whispered, and Mort's joy multiplied, for he understood that she was truly an actress, at all times and in all situations. At the meeting with Henry she had been Rebecca of Sunnybrook Farm, or just plain *Rebecca*. Now she was the temptress from a DeMille sin-and-salvation epic. She was acting like he was irresistible, and making him believe it. They sank onto the couch in a passionate clutch, and every move and sound she made enticed him further. In his arms her body was completely pliant. He fondled her breasts through the satin blouse and she caught her breath. He kissed her throat and she responded with a low animal moan.

But then someone was yelling in the hall. "Sally, are you coming? Are you coming? Sally!" The couch was too narrow to really fit on, and he was sitting on the hem of his coat, which was binding his shoulders. And when he squeezed her, he could feel ribs under his fingers, hard and bony, like a refugee. And still she urged him on.

But it was no use. Once the refugee image entered his mind he saw the army newsreels of the concentration camps, the emaciated bodies, the skeletal corpses. He knew that actresses starved themselves to be able to project an alluring image. But an image is to be looked at, not to be taken in one's arms and . . .

Besides, she was too willing. No challenge. No conquest. Mort lived for the conquest, to rip from weaker hands the prized possession. He straightened up a little, and she knew what it meant. She had offered herself to him without explanation, and he had refused. No further words were necessary. She was relaxed and affectionate, cuddling against him like a child.

But something had been consummated.

Anna

ANNA PAUSED FOR a moment. It had been a long journey from the terrors of the war, the bombings, the fateful train that never arrived in Salzburg, the collapse of Berlin, the Soviet occupation, the escape to the American sector. In some ways the first few months of peace had been worse than the war. But an avant-garde artistic movement sprouted quickly in Berlin, and Anna helped with, and acted in, the first commercial film made after the surrender. Then she and her family had made their way to Frankfurt, where Anna had met Ferdie, an American soldier. She had gone on to Paris, had married Ferdie when he left the army, and come with him to the U.S.

She had done all this to stand now, an émigré actress with four films of experience, on a very warm California winter day, before a small, cheaply built wooden . . . *hut* was the word that came to mind, one of several such buildings gathered around a worn-out patch of grass in the Culver City studio property. In front of the cottage a painted board on two square legs read PUBLICITY DEPT.

Anna was both young and experienced, both supple and hard. She had just come from another building in which she had spent two hours working with an elocution coach on her English pronunciation. It had not gone too badly. The coach was efficient and helpful, and they had tried especially hard to improve Anna's *th*. She was already aware of her tendency to lisp this—*zis*—sound and she was confident she could master it.

Now she had to go to Publicity, and here she felt less certain. She was eighteen when she made that first movie in the ashes of Berlin. The German film industry at that time barely qualified as an industry. The films were small, innovative, questioning movies made by struggling artists for a shattered, disillusioned society. There had been no publicity, no stars, no tours, no press agents. The producers had struggled to buy film stock. The technicians had cursed the broken-down and second-rate equipment that kept malfunctioning.

But now here she was. She walked up the gravel path and opened the door of the hut.

She saw a man sitting on a couch, hunched awkwardly forward over a coffee table. He was attacking a huge sandwich that was more or less falling apart in his hands, dripping mayonnaise and bits of tomato and meat onto a paper plate. The man looked up at Anna and a grunt emerged from his distended cheeks and greasy lips.

Anna's discomfort grew. "Mr. Albert?"

The man held up a finger and masticated quickly and powerfully until the load in his cheeks disappeared. He wiped his fingers and mouth with a shredded napkin. "Yes," he finally said. "Call me Albie."

"I was sent—"

Albie held up a finger again, still chewing and swallowing the last remnants in his mouth. He took a swig of coffee from a paper cup and wiped his lips once more. "Yes, yes. Miss Andres-a-whiskey."

"Andrzejewski."

"Yes, go ahead and have a seat." He indicated a chair on the other side of the coffee table. "Welcome to Hollywood."

Anna could not tell if this simple greeting was sincere or a jest. Albie was a thin man who did not fill out the collar of his shirt, and he had a somewhat rueful expression—when he wasn't gorging himself—that made his welcome hard to read.

He reached over to the nearby desk and picked up a file folder and a writing pad. "First I have to know your life story. Where you're from—obviously Europe, but where exactly?

Where were you born?"

Anna felt uncomfortable talking about her past because it set her apart even more. "In Danzig, which used to be Germany. It's part of Poland now."

"Mm-hmm." He moved some things around on the table until he found a pencil which was hiding under the paper plate. "So you are Polish?"

"That is my ancestry, but I also speak German and have relatives who consider themselves German."

"And you also speak English." Again the slightly arched eyebrow and slightly irreverent tone.

"Not well." Was he making fun? "I try."

"So. Your name is pretty much unpronounceable to Americans. Say it again?"

"Andrzejewski. Ahn-jray-ev-ski."

"Okay." Albert tapped the pad with his pencil. "Mr. Blackwell wants it changed."

"No."

Albie the publicity man looked at Anna with a mixture of surprise and admiration. "I've got a list here. How do you feel about Andrews? An-n-n-drews."

"No. I will keep my name. I already have a career in Europe under that name."

"Your career." Now he was obviously mocking her.

"Yes. Americans will know from my name that I am different. I am an import. Like Dietrich. Like Chevalier. They learned to say that, I feel."

"But it's very common to change one's name." Albie smiled. "Joan Crawford did it. Cary Grant. You know the Andrews sisters? They—"

"No, I don't know them."

Albie stared at her with questioning eyebrows. "You know, *Boogie Woogie, My Dear Mister Shane*. They weren't Andrews, they were Andreyevich or something."

Anna had stumbled over his last sentence. Bookeywookie . . ? She just repeated, "No."

He looked at his list. "Chekhov? How about Anna Che-khov?"

Anna laughed. "Why not Anna Karenina? I did not change my name for the Nazis or for the Russians. So."

Albert shook his head and again Anna caught a glint of frustration and awe. "We can come back to that. Let's fill in the bio. So, born in Danube?"

"Danzig."

"Is that in Sweden? You kind of have that Sonya Haney look."

"It was known as Danzig Free State. It had been part of Prussia, Germany, until the First World War. There was a large German population—"

"But you are Polish?"

"I am Kashubian. I have ancestors from a small—"

"Kashubian."

Having to explain this again gave Anna a frustrated, helpless feeling. Could she ever possibly be accepted here? "It's a small province or country that gets invaded or handed over to whatever other country. Russia, Prussia—"

"I believe you, sweetheart, but nobody knows that here." Albie looked longingly at the scraps of soggy bread on the plate, and Anna felt a little sorry for having interrupted his lunch only to be so difficult.

Priscilla

IT WAS FOR the sake of Priscilla and her sister that their parents bought a theatre in Sioux Falls, so the girls wouldn't grow up on the road, backstage, in train station waiting rooms. The Rivoli was a popular stop for traveling shows of all kinds, from vaudeville to classical, and Priscilla and Veronica helped with the mundane tasks and also frequently filled in or took roles in plays. When Priscilla graduated from high school, her parents insisted she go to college and try to build a normal life, be a normal girl. She tried. She took home economics and French and world history. But after a year she let her parents know that if they would not pay for her to go to New York and study acting, she would do it on her own. They paid. Some.

And there she met Kenny Preston. After the wobbles of that first summer, he had to prove himself to Priscilla. And he had, starting with meeting her parents when they came to New York that fall. They hadn't held a grudge, and Priscilla assumed Kenny had paid her father back, though she never heard about it directly from either one.

They auditioned for plays, he more successfully than she, but not much more. He had the ability to project both tenderness and intensity. It had to do with his eyes. She knew all about eyes. That's the first thing they always said to her, the producers, the agents. *Your eyes!* Or, *those deep, dark, eyes,* or even *those bewitching pools,* when they'd had too much to drink, or too much to think.

Ken didn't have her experience. But what he did have was an equal ambition, and an intense interest in her. He lived in the Village with a cousin or a friend that he never talked about. In fact he almost never spoke of his family or his past, which gave an imbalance to their conversations for awhile, since Priscilla was constantly referring to her parents, her sister, and her hometown friends. But Ken had a sweetness and an otherworldly quality that was both intriguing and mysterious. It seemed that at every step in their relationship, when she arrived at it, he was already there, waiting patiently for her to see what he already saw, to know what he knew. It was almost annoying, but how could she resist?

The fact was, she couldn't. And, of course, when she realized that, there he was, waiting.

"I can't afford a ring," he told her. "I know it's important. And I don't want to give you something cheap."

"I have a ring. My grandmother's. But it's at home. But that's not the problem. I couldn't elope. My parents would be heartbroken."

"Mine would be mad. They already think my life is a mistake."

He could not possibly afford a ring, and she could not possibly accept a proposal, but he did, she did, and one glorious whirlwind day, a year and three months after meeting, they did. Then her entire future was shared equally and completely with him. They both saw themselves in the theatre, the New York theatre, of course. Her ideal was Katharine Cornell, his was Luther Adler. They would go to Hollywood when Hollywood called, they decided, for the money, for the challenge, but they would always come back to live theatre.

These are the dreams that young, ambitious people share—ambitious not just professionally, but for everything. For blazing romance, for eternal love, for deep meaning and day-to-day joy, for wonderful, happy children and witty friends and Algonquin Round Table and climbing Mount Everest. And Ken and Priscilla shared these dreams.

Priscilla had great talent, but also great insecurity. She

could do wonderfully well in the hands of a strong but patient director. And she was very ambitious. In her small-town theatre days she had met performers who were brilliant. "But," she told Ken, "They were utterly unknown beyond whatever their particular circuit might be—Keokuk to Lansing to Louisville to God Knows Where."

His eyes shone with conviction. "I would never do that."

"Never!" she agreed.

"Except as a last resort." And they burst into laughter. Anyone who knew anything about theatre knew they were describing their most likely future.

They completed their second year at the Academy, and then it was time to go to work. No going home now, no summer playhouse. They tramped, together and separately, all over the hard, dusty sidewalks of Manhattan to auditions, to agents, to offices and cafes and show-biz hangouts. If you sat around in certain places with certain people, you heard leads, rumors and wild speculation among the crowd of those hoping to do what you were hoping to do. To get the Big Break.

Ken hit first, because he had the right look to be cast as a juvenile, a young man long on energy and short on under-standing. He was also good enough on radio to get a supporting role on a continuing soap opera. Priscilla, on the other hand, largely because of those large, dark eyes and a naturally voluptuous figure, had trouble being seen as an ingenue, an innocent girl, but her face was too fresh-looking to play the soubrette, the saucy wench, or her modern descendent, the mantrap, the showgirl, the dolly, the baby. And this was all about image, not ability. Priscilla felt she could play any good role, given the opportunity, that she could outshine, or at least compete with, any actress her age. But the agents and producers were as dull-witted as they were avaricious. And lascivious, of course. At the age of twenty, she could afford to be patient. By twenty-two, less so. By twenty-three, the patience in the account was seriously depleted.

✧   ✧   ✧

BUT THEN ALONG came a man who fell in love not just with her eyes and her body but with all of her. Of course, he was utterly mad, with an impetuousness that went way past anything Kenny had. He was also powerful. The most powerful man in Hollywood.

She had no clue. Why would she even suspect? After all, this was New York. She had come to a cattle call for a show she knew little about, by a female playwright, to judge by the name, that Priscilla had never heard of. That skinny chain-smoking woman in the middle of the house would be her.

Priscilla was a veteran of New York showbiz by this time. So she was used to the casual chaos of an audition. They call you in, you get talked at or ignored by various people, not knowing who is important. Then they gave you a feather of hope to cling to and shove you out the door.

But this time Morton was there, leaning over and talking to the lady playwright from the row behind. At first he was just some guy, but Priscilla did register a brown plaid jacket with a thin, yellow thread in the pattern. The stage manager told her to wait. That was a good sign.

While sitting around with some others in the left wing, she saw that unusual plaid again, coming toward her now, and she noticed the face of the man wearing it. He was big, sturdy, with wavy dark hair combed back. He had small, piercing eyes behind rimless spectacles, and the eyes were trained on her in a way that made her both uncomfortable and hopeful. She later felt that it was a good thing she did not recognize him. That would have made her much more nervous. By the time she found out who he was, she knew him too well to be shy.

He asked her to coffee and Priscilla, thinking this was why she had been told to wait, went across the street with him to a drugstore. She chose the booth by the window and slid in just far enough, so he would not think of trying to sit next to her. You never know. He sat opposite, lit a cig. Asked the preliminary questions. Where from? How old? Been in theatre?

She filled in the bio. A boy in a white apron brought the coffee.

"Any Indian in you?"

He was certainly direct. "No."

"You have these beautiful cheekbones." He touched his own cheeks, as if in explanation.

If he was just some guy—say the boy in the apron—she would have laughed, he was being so gloriously simple. But he was not just some guy. He obviously had something to do with the play, though she wasn't sure what. He acted like he wrote it, or owned it. She smiled. "Yes, I've heard that. But as far as I know all my ancestors were English and Welsh."

She gave him a short travelogue of her life, up to arriving in New York.

He cut her off. "You got some talent, but this play, it's not for you. You've got a dramatic heroine in you, waiting to come out."

"I . . . I what?" It was one of the most extraordinary things anyone had ever said to her. "Really? But you hardly saw me."

"I'd like to see more. You remind me of Vivien Leigh."

Priscilla laughed, in spite of herself. "I'd like to be Vivien Leigh."

He shook his head, frowning with what seemed like disdain. "No, you wouldn't. She's . . . well, trust me, you wouldn't."

She laughed again, and this time didn't try to stifle it.

Maybe he *was* just another guy, another forty-year-old guy in a flashy sport coat, on the make. It didn't help that the next thing he said was, "Have you ever thought about movies?"

Priscilla was simply too kind a person to give him the sarcastic reply that was on the tip of her tongue. She said, "Well, of course! But you have to start somewhere."

"Indeed." He lapsed into silence.

He seemed to be at least trying to be businesslike. But he also was checking her out for other uses. That was obvious and completely unremarkable. Just part of the deal . . . . The Bloodhounds of Broadway. Was that a show or a story she had seen or read, or did she just now make it up? Anyway, that was the way it was. Young women, hopeful actresses, had to have the instincts of a jackrabbit and the determination of a wolverine—both speed and sharp claws—to get anywhere. With this one in the checkered coat, older and more seemingly solid, she would fall back on being a married woman from the midwest—innocent, upright, church-going and all that. With that routine she could probably avoid his clutches.

But on the other hand, if he could do anything for her, she could not let him leave this booth without making some kind of a commitment. Instincts. Agility.

He looked at his watch. "My evening is not free, but I would love to see more of what you can do. Can you come to my hotel tomorrow, say, two o'clock?"

"And what hotel is that?"

"The Waldorf."

"I'm sorry, I'm sure it is, but I've a previous engagement."

"Alright." He looked peeved. "Alright. My agent's office. Two would be great—"

"You are serious."

He actually harumphed. This description was familiar to her, since it seemed to turn up in play scripts with great frequency. "I am always serious," he said. "And I don't hold auditions for fun. So we'll say two?" He reached into his jacket and pulled out a calling card and a fountain pen. He wrote on the blank side of the card. This is my agent's address."

He handed her the card. His scrawl read: *Myron Seitz, 247 W. 47th St.*

She looked up. His gaze had become even more piercing. "Are you married?"

"Yes."

"Husband here in New York?"

"Yes." She wanted to invoke the reality of Ken. "He's in a play at the Cherry Lane in about, oh, forty-five minutes."

"But you're an actress. You want to work."

"Of course."

"You have the ambition and the independence to pursue your own career." He managed a smile. "Sorry, I'm not trying to imply anything, but that drive is something not all married actresses have."

"Well, I've got it, brother."

"Because if I sign you, you will work. Hard and long. And if you succeed, well, the road gets rougher."

He said this in such a matter-of-fact way that for the first time in the conversation Priscilla felt a little buzz of real hope.

✧   ✧   ✧

IT WAS ODD that she did not turn the card over and read his name until she was on the subway headed home.

Morton Blackwell, Blackwell Productions, Hollywood— New York. She knew she had heard the name but couldn't attach it to anything specific. At that point he only represented to her the way to success and happiness for herself, and just as much for Ken.

And Ken certainly knew who he was.

"Are you kidding me?" He laughed with a pent-up enthusiasm for any positive news. "Blackwell! Jesus, kid, that's a pretty big deal. Are you excited?"

"Now I am!"

He hugged her. "Yeah, well, be happy, but, y'know—"

"I know."

He laughed again. "You'll be great. They're going to want you. He's going to want you. Don't worry, do your best, for God and country!"

The audition with Blackwell consisted of a long interview with Morton, the agent Seitz, and a woman named Carla Brown who seemed to act as a sort of sounding board or devil's advocate for Blackwell. Priscilla gave them a reading from a John Howard Lawson play, and the parts of Mary, Sylvia, *and* Crystal from *The Women*. After this workout Priscilla left the office dejected, certain she would never hear from Blackwell again, but the phone was ringing when she walked into the apartment. It was Seitz' secretary. Please come back at ten in the morning.

Priscilla assumed this would be another audition and steeled herself for an ordeal. But when she walked in, only Seitz was there, and the papers he gave her were not a script but a contract. A one-year personal services contract with Morton Blackwell Productions, renewable, for two hundred dollars a week.

Priscilla sat down and asked for a glass of water, which Seitz poured for her. As the daughter of a theater owner, she knew to read the contract carefully. The base pay assured her availability for meetings, readings, screen tests, appearances and just about everything an actor does besides act. She would receive an additional two hundred per week if she spent one or more days of the week in rehearsal or filming as a bit player (five lines or less of dialogue), a total of $750 for any week in which she was playing a featured or supporting role, and $1000 for a lead role.

And there were per diems, and clauses about costume, makeup, travel, personal conduct, publicity, and more. Priscilla read it through. Now that it had come, now that it was in her hands, she felt remarkably clear-eyed and washed clean. Happy but not giddy. Hopeful but calmly realistic.

While she read, Seitz sorted through a stack of mail on the desk. He said, "You can take this home and discuss it with—"

"No. That's alright." Priscilla smiled at him and signed the contract. They shook hands and Priscilla took the elevator down and walked through the door of the building back out onto Forty-Seventh Street into the brisk fall air. Across the street stood the old Mansfield Theatre, where she had once auditioned for some sort of vaudeville, or review— she hadn't been in the building long enough to notice anything but the musty, sawdusty smell.

CHAPTER THREE
March 1947

Lyman

LYMAN WILBUR WAS in his office reading a magazine article about fishing in Iceland—could there possibly be a more uninviting place name?—rather than doing what he was supposed to be doing, which was diving into the pile of scripts on his desk. His telephone rang.

"Hello, Lyman, this's—"

"Good morning, April." He always knew when April Sheffield was on the line. They had something of a past together, and a mutual affinity that went beyond their professional roles at Colosseum Pictures: hers as secretary to a producer, his as a contract writer. Anyway, he always knew her voice as soon as he heard it.

"He wants to see you," she said. "How's ten?"

"I am at your service, or his service. Anybody's service that needs me."

"Alright," she chuckled. "See you then."

At the appointed hour he walked into the office. She was on the phone but waved him past. He poked his head in Sheldrake's door. "You rang for me?"

Fred Sheldrake stood behind a large, polished mahogany desk, talking on the phone. He motioned for Lyman to come in. Lyman shut the door and moved toward a chair. Sheldrake was the first man Lyman had met the day he came to work at Colosseum Pictures, and now he had a feeling, almost grown to a certainty, that Sheldrake would be the last man he saw on the way out. And that today might be the day that happened.

As Lyman took a seat, he saw some papers neatly stacked on the blotter of Sheldrake's desk. Even from six feet away and upside down he recognized these as the script pages he had written a few days ago for *The Message in the Bottle*.

Sheldrake stood there, one hand holding the phone to his ear, the other hand holding a large unlit cigar. He seemed to be not so much listening as waiting to listen. His dark eyes stared at nothing. His bald dome radiated impatience. Finally he muttered a few words and hung up. He sat down in his high-backed swivel chair and stuck the cigar in his mouth.

"I've got good news and bad news." He smiled slightly at this very unoriginal witticism. "The good news is that you have a chance at a very good picture in about three months. The bad news is I'm firing your ass tomorrow. Or the next day."

So there it is, thought Lyman. Feared but not unexpected.

"I come in to your office and find you passed out on the couch at ten o'clock in the morning." Sheldrake waved the cigar at the short stack of lightly pawed papers before him. "And this on your desk."

Lyman did not attempt an explanation. There was nothing to explain. The two men sat quietly, staring at the papers. Sheldrake lit the cigar and held the burning match. Lyman wondered if he would apply it to the papers, but he waved it out and tossed it into the large amber ashtray next to the telephone. From outside came a distant echo of a hammer on nails and wood, probably a set carpenter on one of the nearby sound stages.

"And it's not bad writing," said Sheldrake. "The work is fine. It's the what else that's the problem."

"Yeah," Lyman agreed.

"The drinking is affecting your personality. You pulled this off," he waved at the papers again, "—but it feels like your performance overall is just, well, more and more less and less. Now there's some guys around here who'd say, *if he keeps churning it out, buy him a case!* But I can't agree with that."

Before this wisdom, Lyman was helpless. "So what's the great movie I'm not going to do?"

"Alexander Stowbridge."

Lyman was stunned. Stowbridge! The British wonder boy!

"You would be adapting something for him. Some ghost story or something. We're renting him from Blackwell Studios. Or we could be. It's in the works."

Stowbridge was known as the master of suspense, and his movies were famous for their surprising plots and subtly twisted characters. Lyman felt a twinge of regret for the lost opportunity. "I would be, if . . ."

"You will be, after you make some changes. Starting tomorrow, you have thirty days off. Paid. And you will call this man."

Sheldrake snapped a business card and Lyman leaned across the desk to take it. He looked at the card. The name meant nothing to him.

"Dr. Rosenstone has a lot of experience with alcoholic cases. He did wonders with Tracy."

Talking about drinking had the effect of making Lyman want a drink and realize he was not hung over. He also wondered how Dick Tracy was treated for alcoholism. It was disorienting.

"If I see you around here in the next thirty days, or even hear of you being around, or hear of you drinking in public or in private, you're fired. The form is already filled out." Sheldrake patted the desk with his right palm, apparently indicating the drawer beneath which held the deadly termination notice. "And if I ever thereafter find you drunk or drinking on these premises, also shit-canned."

Lyman sighed at this completely arbitrary dilemma. "And if I'm a good little doggie I get to be on a good job and make good money."

Sheldrake smiled that broad pilgrim-jawed smile of his and stuck the cigar into the side of it.

"The fact is," continued Lyman. "I haven't had a drop in three days, or four."

Sheldrake's grin melted into a pitying glance. "Look, I know. It's been tough on you, missing your wife. But it's been several months and we're still scraping you off the floor with a spatula."

Annoyed, Lyman began to repeat, "I haven't had—"

"Yeah, three days. And I bet you could tell me how many hours. Look, you're not the first. Some of the biggest, nicest . . ." Sheldrake held the cigar before him and admired the ribbon of smoke rising from it. "Reformed drunks. It's almost a badge of honor. It would probably help my career." He shrugged.

With great reluctance, Lyman admitted to himself that he would try to do what the man wanted. After all, he had once spent thirteen years pretty much on the wagon, the best thirteen years of his life. So he could do another six months. The carrot in front of his face was a tasty one. Alexander Stowbridge was considered a director's director, quirky but brilliant, and never a false step. That Cary Grant thriller that just came out, with whatshername, that was Stowbridge. And all his movies made money, and his writers gained fame and won awards.

Lyman's burst of resolve was quickly pierced by a stab of despair. What would be the point? To which of the three cats in the house would he read the glowing reviews? To what silent piece of furniture would he show the award he'd won? This man was taking away his scotch—forever! That could not be allowed!

Lyman caught himself. The addiction that ruled his life was now on notice, and it would do anything, tell him anything, to regain control. This was going to be a battle. He slumped in his chair, utterly discouraged. "You have obviously mistaken me," he growled, "for a person of character and willpower."

"Obviously." Sheldrake pushed a button on his squawk box. "Did you drive here?"

"Yeah, why?" Lyman felt the door behind him open. He did not look around.

Sheldrake said, "Miss Sheffield, we'll have that car now."

Lyman heard the door softly close. "What's the car for?"

"To take you home. You're staying at the Roosevelt Hotel?"

Lyman shook his head. "The Sunset Tower, but I'm quite capable."

"No," Sheldrake was firm. "I insist. And what I want, I'm going to get. Or—" He patted the desk again.

"Lord!" Lyman stood up. April stood waiting by the door. She gave him a quick, professional, insincere smile. Sheldrake watched him impassively. Lyman said, "Thanks, Fred."

"You'll hate me in the morning."

Lyman chuckled, in spite of everything. "I hate you now."

He followed April out onto the studio street. She turned and gave him a warm, familiar, sincere smile.

Lyman stopped in front of her. "April, April. Did you have something to do with this?"

"No, but it's a good idea." She brushed a speck off his shoulder. "I really hope you'll—"

"Don't." He put up his hand. "Just don't."

She gave him that patented warm, half-teasing expression, the one that said *I'm your friend, think of me like a daughter, or a loyal secretary. Just not your secretary*. "I can't stand to see you so unhappy. And, like this."

She meant staggering drunk. "I haven't had a drop in sixty hours."

She ignored that. "And I know she would—"

"Be very disappointed in me."

"No, she would wish you to do this." April doled out another smile. "To, you know, take this chance. This opportunity."

Lyman had a complicated, familiar relationship with April. Complicated by his sexual attraction to her, an attraction that would never go anywhere because he was fifty-four, a pudgy, irritable lush, and she was a pretty, smart, happy young woman who had her whole life in front of her.

"Well," said Lyman. "It's an easy thing to wish. I wish it myself. But a devilishly hard thing to do."

The black studio car pulled up. April pulled open the passenger door.

"I like your chances," she said. She kissed him on the cheek and grasped his hand as he slid into the car. "Good luck."

THE NEXT MORNING, Lyman sat in another office, this one in Beverly Hills, on a soft leather couch, wondering if the leather was pigskin and whether the doctor who sat in the chair cornerwise was Jewish. He assumed the answer in both cases to be yes, and therefore, was the couch kosher? These thoughts stumbled through his mind and were quickly forgotten. Lyman was not having a good morning.

Dr. Rosenstone had straight dark gray hair parted severely on the right side of his head. He had a natural tan and pale, dry-looking lips. His eyes were always busy—a professional snoop, thought Lyman.

"I've arranged a place for you at the Ashton Clinic in Sherman Oaks. It's a damn fine place. You'll have your own room. The grounds are lovely. It's more like a farm than a sanitarium, really. There's a full-time med staff." The doctor's smile was meant to be somewhere in the neighborhood of encouraging and reassuring. "This is the dry-out. You spend a couple of weeks there, I'll come and see how you're doing, but we won't start intensive sessions until you're released. You're getting rid of your crutches, so you will have to learn to walk again. I will help you do that."

Lyman nodded. What was there to say?

"How are you feeling now?" he asked. "When was the last time you had a—"

"I had a weak whisky and soda for breakfast. Just to steady my nerves."

"I see."

"À la Churchill."

Rosenstone betrayed no amusement at Lyman's attempted levity. "Yes, so they say. You have a history of abstinence and relapse."

"Oh yes. A history. Almost an archaeology." Lyman's humor did not arise from a newborn sense of fun, but rather from nervousness. He awoke this morning on the floor of his hotel, still drunk. The breakfast whisky at the hotel bar was needed as much to steady his hands as his nerves. Even as the doctor spoke to him in that smooth, superior baritone, Lyman was giving half his somewhat impaired attention to the idea of just getting up and walking out.

But he wondered about the Stowbridge project, which had glimmered intriguingly in the back of his mind since he heard about it. What must it be like to work for someone who combined the rarity of actual artistry with the too-common artistic temperament?

The doctor was contemplating him with a trace of a smile, and Lyman realized he had been asked a question, and, a second later, what the question was. "No," he replied, "no one."

"Brothers, sisters, friends?"

"Most of my friends are pen pals. We seldom discuss personal matters."

"Has your drinking increased since your wife's passing?"

"I think you know the answer to that. It's why I'm here."

"Indeed." A flash of a professional perfunctory smile. "Do you suffer from loneliness?"

Lyman fought off a little swell of indignation. "I have always suffered from it. The definition of loneliness implies that it is not a happy state."

Rosenstone chuckled, at last. "You're a writer. You use words as tools and as playthings."

"And you are a psychiatrist. From what I know of that art, you use words as therapy. As a cure."

Dr. Rosenstone

DR. ROSENSTONE PAUSED. There was that word again.

"We treat," he said. "We don't cure."

Lyman Wilbur nodded. He was the screenwriter who had been referred by his studio.

Robert Rosenstone, or Doc Rosenstone, as he was known to friends, colleagues, and longtime patients, had trained in Vienna in the 1920s and then been a teacher at the New England Psychoanalytic Institute. But he was originally from Albuquerque, and in 1938, tired of the professional infighting and personal politics of the Eastern psychiatric hive and depressed over his recent divorce, he had reestablished himself in the warmth and relative peace of Los Angeles.

He had found movie people to be quite open to analysis. Writers, producers, execs, and actors seemed to fall into natural categories of neurosis and frustration. The actors had to deal with their innately narcissistic profession, with questions about their sexuality, the pressures of constantly being onstage, and, almost always, some sort of inferiority complex. The producers and execs, though as a class more neurotic than the actors, often as not seemed to be looking for ways to use psychoanalytical concepts to control others, or maybe even to control fate. And psychiatry had become a new obsession for everyone in theatre and movies as a dramatic device or theme: all the young actors and writers and hopeful directors who couldn't afford actual treatment had become amateur experts in it. When those young people got a contract and made some money, getting onto a psychiatrist's couch was one of the first ways a lot of them found to spend it.

Of course, some of these people were in great pain and

confusion, willing to try anything for relief from their personal demons. These tended to be mainly the sexually confused, and the alcoholics. Here was the meat of psychoanalysis, beyond the humdrum of unsatisfied wives and frustrated career men. Almost always the homosexual, the Casanova, the addict, the fetishist, the Svengali sprang from repressed, traditional families, and plumbing the caverns of those minds and those families was the true mission of Freud's followers.

The writer who sat before him seemed to be such a hard case. A lifelong alcoholic, he seemed also likely to be a repressed homosexual, possibly with a mother complex. Such types, especially, often showed up looking for a cure. Or better stated, The Cure.

And so it went.

"No, there won't be a cure, I'm glad to say. What is going to happen is that, through various techniques, we will find the sinkhole that you keep trying to fill with whiskey and gin. And you are right, it's all about words. But I think of words in therapy as smoke signals. Metaphorically speaking, I am at some distance away. The smoke tells me that there is someone out here, in the forest. It tells me if there is fear, or a desire to meet, and where to find you, and how I might help. The treatment comes from within you. It is your work, and your accomplishment, not mine."

"Yes, words." For the first time there was a spark of interest in Wilbur's florid, blotchy face. "All that separate us from the animals. Or the vegetables, for that matter. We must speak. There is no human group that does not have a language." He cast a suspicious glance at the doctor. "You're not one of those back-to-the-uterus types, are you?"

Rosenstone had to laugh. "No. I am a psychoanalyst. But the science has evolved since Freud. Like Columbus, he discovered a new continent. But after him came Picasso and Cortez and De Soto—"

"Picasso? Isn't he the painter?"

The "slip" had been intentional. Rosenstone had many tricks in his Satchmo. He chuckled. "Did I say Picasso? Well, so there. I may be somewhat out of my depth trying to get all literary."

Wilbur shrugged. "Well, Shakespeare got the Hamlet story wrong. It happens to the best."

Rosenstone moved on. "You were nominated, weren't you? For that Deborah Boynton picture? *Double Up? Double Dare?*"

Wilbur gave him a resentful glance, apparently offended. How dare I bring up your Academy Award nomination!

"Yeah," he muttered. "*Double Down.* I was nominated with Max Beckerman, for the screenplay."

Rosenstone said, "I must tell you, that was an excellent picture. One of the few that portrayed sexuality as something more than romance or melodrama."

"Well, it was based on my first novel, which. . . I mean, any psychology in it was right off the street, people I'd have bumped shoulders with in any train station or grocery store or saloon."

"I could see that," Rosenstone said. "It dealt with some interesting concepts—at least as much as a detective movie can."

"Really? In what way?"

"Well, the idea of the sex object as death wish. The Black Widow. Look but don't touch. The supposedly cynical guy who turns out to be a sucker."

Wilbur chuckled. "He does indeed."

"And Deborah Boynton is always fascinating. At least, from what we, the gullible public hear." Yes, Rosenstone admitted to being a little starstruck himself, but he was always on the lookout for well-known clients to add to his stable.

"I did meet her, to my regret."

Rosenstone decided against pursuing that story for now.

"What else have you worked on?"

"Aside from writing my fourth novel and starting another one, nothing of note. My work in pictures has been desultory and, uh, well, it pays the bills." He was getting noticeably antsy now. "So, it's off to the D.T. ward for me."

Rosenstone had heard enough for one day. "A necessary but hopefully not too uncomfortable part of the process."

Lyman Wilbur closed his eyes and pulled his head back. He rubbed his forehead with the tips of his fingers.

"Alright," he said.

Priscilla

PRISCILLA'S KNOCK WAS answered by "Come on in Cilla." She opened the door. Mrs. B was running a carpet sweeper over the living room rug. "Had a little accident," she said. She glanced up at Priscilla. "Kept you late this evening?"

"Oh, God!" Priscilla slumped her shoulders as if exhausted, then popped back up, smiling.

"I warned you!" Mrs. B. shook her head. "Come on in."

The boy stared at her sleepily from the couch.

"We just had our tea," said Mrs. B.

"Oh, shoot." That was what Priscilla had come for, tea and sympathy.

"Don't worry, there's still plenty." Mrs. B. picked up Greggy like a large, limp doll and carried him toward the bedroom, Priscilla said, "I never get to see your son awake."

"Count yourself lucky." She glanced back over her shoulder and continued down the hall. Priscilla went into the kitchen, where she could see the teacups and spoons on the table. Mrs. Brown lived with the boy and a housekeeper in a spacious home not far from the studio, Priscilla had become a frequent visitor. She ran some water into the tea kettle and set it on the stove to heat.

Mrs. B. returned just as the kettle was beginning to whistle. "You hungry, dear?"

"No, no. I've been eating snacks all day." Priscilla had been shooting the scene where she has a heartfelt conversation with the priest played by Brett Walsh, except he was off somewhere. So she spoke the lines to a point three feet in front of her eyes. But as she was doing this, she could see Mort standing at the edge of the light with his arms clasped across his chest. She could tell he didn't like something. And, sure enough, they took a break and Mort wrote a new scene while Priscilla went for coffee and a roll. An hour or so later they did the new lines.

Then they rehearsed a scene in the little kitchen set, but there was difficulty with the camera placement in relation to the table and the fireplace. Mort had a spirited discussion with Henry, the director. Another break while the crew moved furniture and cut a hole in a wall for the camera to peek through. More sitting around, not restful at all because of the tension and stress that radiated out from Mort like . . . Priscilla was too tired to come up with the thing that radiated out from Mort like.

Mrs. B. turned off the stove. "So, cup o' tea? I've got some jasmine, and the passion flower."

Priscilla had a change of mind. "No, better make it coffee. I don't need to relax tonight, I just need to get home."

Mrs. B. gave her one of her warm, understanding smiles, and brought down two clean cups and the jar of Nescafé. Priscilla scooped out the portions while Mrs. B.sat down across from her, groaning slightly.

"*You've* had the tough day, Carla," said Priscilla.

"No, no, not really. Just age catching up."

"It must be tough with Greggy."

"No, not most days. But I'm lucky to have Plambeck. She really takes charge, and she loves Greggy. And Mort insists that I go home at regular closing time. He understands how important it is." She sipped her coffee. "How's your love life?"

Priscilla didn't mind the nosy question. It was just a humorous way of asking about Ken. "Still in New York till the season ends."

"I'm sure that'll be a big relief to you."

"I'm looking forward to it." Priscilla said. This was an untruth. The thought of Ken's return filled her with both hope and dread. She changed the subject. "Do you think

Henry's going to make it to the end of the picture?"

"Yeah, he'll be fine. He's worked for Mort before. He's used to what Mort's like. Everyone knows this pic is a home run ball. We all want to knock it out of the park. Then you get to be a star."

"Instead of the big secret."

"Again, Mort being Mort."

"Has he always been like this?"

"He sure has his ups and down. This is up, by the way."

At the announcement of the picture in January, Mort had refused to give the press her name, which at that point was still Priscilla Preston. As filming went on and she became Pamela Carr, the publicity department had released little bits of information about her, focusing on her youth and innocent beauty and strongly implying, it seemed to Priscilla, that she was somewhere around seventeen years old and had been plucked right off an Iowa—Iowa!—farm. Since her name was newly minted, no one could find any trace of the actress who'd knocked around New York for three years, appearing in choruses and crowd scenes, walking on and off stages, with a credit at the bottom of the page if it was given at all. "But I don't want to be a star," she said. "I just want to be an actress."

"Focus on the task at hand." Mrs. B. used her napkin to wipe a wet spot on the yellow-painted table. "Stay in the center of yourself. In today. Don't worry about tomorrow. It'll be here soon enough. And don't regret yesterday. It'll always be there."

"That's great advice."

"What you really need is a flower garden. Getting down on my knees in the dirt does wonders for me. Caring about something that's alive, and real. These are things I've learned."

"So when I have this big success, that'll be the first thing I buy, is a garden." They both chuckled, but Priscilla really meant it. She considered Mrs. B. a sterling example in both work and life. "Everything you do down there, and then taking care of a home, of your son—"

"Well, I've got it pretty easy, truth be told. I'm home at six every night. And Mort takes care of all the therapy and bills."

"Thanks for the invite," she said.

"You seemed like you needed someone to talk to."

"Yes," she said, "I need to get out of there once in a while."

Mrs. B. reached over and patted Priscilla's hand. "It's not easy."

Without naming it, they both knew what was being discussed. On weeknights, after filming, Mort might come by Priscilla's hotel at any time. The man never seemed to sleep. Sometimes he just wanted to talk. Sometimes he wanted sex, fast and crude. But then he might lie with her for an hour as she whispered her life story to him until she fell asleep. Then he would be gone. This was a new kind of love for her, but she knew it was love. Against all intention and common sense. It was the very thing she has sworn she would never do. And it was a trap. Priscilla was married. Mort was married. It was a love with no tomorrow.

In the drawer of the nightstand next to where this adultery was taking place lay folded letters from her husband telling of his devotion, his eagerness to rejoin her, and his plans for their future. Kenny would be coming to California by the first of May, as soon as the radio show he was working on wrapped up the season. Priscilla was uncertain whether the filming of *Angeline* would be completed by then. She had not decided, *could* not decide, what would happen then. She would have to start living with Ken, wouldn't she? But she would continue the affair with Morton, shouldn't she? She was happier now, and more fulfilled than ever in her life. She was also more anxious and uncertain than she had ever been.

Mrs. B. knew about her relationship with Mort because she knew about everything. At times it seemed like she was really the one in charge in the organization. At least Mort listened to her with a quiet attention he didn't often give to anyone else, even Priscilla. She did not pretend she could solve Priscilla's love dilemma. But at least she listened.

"Well," Mrs. B. sipped her coffee. "Sometimes he just has to be told *no*. I do it in the daytime, Elaine does it at night, and you need to do it, too."

"I can't. I don't feel like I have the right."

The older woman stared at Priscilla for a long moment. "Tell you what. . ." She stood up and retrieved a pencil and notepad from a one of the drawers. "Sometimes it helps to talk to . . . I want you to talk to this man I know. He's a, I don't know what you call him. A counselor. A wise man. An advisor. He's kind, and smart, and he knows the business." She wrote something on the paper and showed it to Priscilla: *Rosenstone for P.* "I'll set it up so you can go see him next week."

Priscilla felt very lucky to have a friend like Mrs. Brown, who always seemed to know exactly what to do.

Anna

SHE HAD HAD not heard anything from the studio for a week, but then Anna received a call from a lady in Mr. Blackwell's office, who told her to come into the studio for tests and meetings. She had to find her way through the complex to a large building, and within that to the hair salon, where she was greeted warmly by a chain-smoking lady with green eyes and very short lacquered bangs. The lady looked in a folder, and then she washed and clipped Anna's hair with great care before handing Anna the folder and directing her to a room down the hall where her makeup was scrubbed off and redone. Then she was sent a few doors farther down to a photographer's studio where she sat for a while.

While waiting, she looked through the folder. It contained headshots of several young women. Anna assumed that these were examples of how her hair and makeup were to be done. There was also a dossier giving her height, weight, dress size, shoe size, etc. Not all the information was correct.

Finally a photographer called her in and put her through a lengthy sitting in various costumes while the hairdresser, the makeup artist and the wardrobe woman stood around and studied her from various angles. Between cigarettes, one of them would come to Anna and make an adjustment, a touchup, a pat of the hair. The photographer directed her to different poses and expressions. He was very enthusiastic, but his instructions were delivered in a kind of sing-song, with expressions she had never heard before. She was not a professional model, and felt utterly inadequate. She did her best to imitate the facial expressions he mimed while talking. It was stressful and exhausting.

After about an hour, the photographer told her they were through. By now lunchtime had come and gone, but Anna didn't care. Her greater hunger was to act in a movie, and she understood that in Hollywood this would be a long, slow, relentless series of steps.

When she came out of the dressing room, the photographer held up her folder. "Last stop for you today is the whatcha call it. You know where MGM is?"

Anna felt a little tremor of excitement. She didn't know where MGM was, but she surely knew what it was.

"You have to go over there." He handed her a slip of paper. "It's just, turn left on Washington and you can practically see it. The office entrance is like a half-mile down. Did you drive?"

"No."

"It's really not far. You're supposed to ask for Mrs. Copelan."

"Is this an audition?"

"I really don't know."

Not knowing when she would get out, Anna had planned to take the bus home and knew where the bus stop was and not much else. On Washington, she had to go left, he had said. So she started out. It had been cool and foggy in the morning, now the sky was overcast, and the air was warm, with a dank sort of harbor aroma.

As she walked, what struck her forcefully, again, was the buildings. They came from every era of the city's history, from frontier days to art moderne of the thirties, with a lot of Mexican-type style mixed in.

And they were all still standing. By the end in Berlin, whole sections of town had been knocked into stacks and piles, which people seldom bothered with except where they had to be moved out of the street. At that point it did not matter if the building was a castle from the sixteenth century or the lowliest lunch stand. All were equal under the bombs.

Some neighborhoods came out much better off and people lived there in any spare space that could be found, usually with strangers. One's family, at that point, was the people you survived the night with.

Anna followed the house numbers up the street. As they approached 10,000, she wondered what happened after that. Ahead stood the entrance to MGM, but the number she was looking for was on the opposite side of the street. It was a three story office building, the Dorchester Building, with marble floors and wainscoting. A directory in the small foyer said "Copelan Office: 105." It was the back office on the first floor, and she could see the door was open.

Anna walked over and peered hesitantly into the well-lit office. On the back wall hung a framed sign: JEWISH COMMUNITY COMMITTEE. Anna straightened up, surprised and a little frightened. What was this?

A man looked up from the desk. "Yes, miss?"

"I am sent to meet Mrs. Copelan. From the studio." She had never been more aware of her German accent.

But the man smiled and said, "Yes, of course. *Bist du kurzlich vorbei gekommen?*"

This friendly greeting frightened Anna even more. "I don't know why I'm here. I'm Anna Andrzejewski. Blackstone sent me."

He arched an eyebrow. "You mean Blackwell?"

"Yes, of course. Blackwell."

"Yes, come in." He stood up, a short, burly man with very short hair. "No one has explained this to you?"

"No."

"We are a civic group, and our mission is to prevent the spread of Nazism into the studios. We ask to interview German and other immigrants to accomplish that goal and to help you get oriented to this country. It's very simple."

"Well, no worry there. I'm certainly not a Nazi."

"A fact which we will ascertain." He smiled again and

seemed kind and genuine.

A few minutes later she was sitting at a table with the man, Schwartz, and a women, not named Copelan but Mrs. Sherman. A short, wiry woman with a strained smile. They were Jewish, of course, but they said that what they were doing had nothing to do with religion or race. It was simply a matter of security.

First they told her their stories. Schwartz had come from Berlin as a young man in the early thirties, before the Nazis took power. "Back when coming here was *looking for opportunity*, not *escaping*." Sherman had had a very frightening journey, stowing away on a ship to Brazil, then working her way to Mexico, and finally to the U.S.

Anna remembered the anger and fear she had felt as the Jews who had been her neighbors in Danzig had fled when Nazis gained control of the city government, even before the invasion of Poland. Telling this to the man and the woman now, she could not help but be aware that an actual Nazi would be saying the same thing.

"And when we arrived in Berlin, well, it was . . . we were somewhat refugees ourselves."

"But you still supported the party." Mrs. Sherman rolled a pencil between her fingers. "And the state."

"It was suicide not to. No one was safe. There were spies and informers everywhere. By then, of course the party apparatus was primarily old ladies and schoolchildren. But still."

Schwartz said, "And where did you work?"

"I was in school. When graduated I was accepted into the apprenticeship program at UFA.

"The film studio."

"That must have been hard to get. Who helped you get in?"

"No one. I applied. All I did at first was make drawings and paintings. The only other place I worked was helping out in my mother's shoe shop."

"Did you witness atrocities?"

"I'm not familiar—"

"*Grausamkeiten.*" The woman bit off the word. "Brutal and violent acts against citizens, against anybody."

Anna felt a deep stab in her gut. "Of course." They sat there waiting for more. "People were beaten and taken away, their homes looted." She had a very clear image of a boy, maybe twelve, with his arms wrapped around a heavy wooden gramophone, almost as big as he was, struggling down the steps from an apartment, a joyous grin on his face.

"But you were still a party member."

"No. They gave you forms to fill out. Everyone filled them out. You were watched constantly. But I never went to meetings, I never served in the apparatus. And I avoided people who did. It was possible to keep a low profile, and find others who were doing the same."

Anna shuddered. She had never grown inured to the bloody chaos of those times. "And the bombs fell. Every day."

"And then the Russians came." Sherman twirled the pencil. They both had papers on the table in front of them, but Anna had not seen either one write anything down.

"Yes."

"What happened to you?"

"Nothing. I survived."

"Nothing?" Sherman frowned. "A beautiful young girl like you?"

Anna knew that she was talking about the rapes. That was the actual brutality that had come closest to her. The first wave of Russians had come in like the Cossacks most of them were. Taking what they wanted, doing what they wanted. Even killing who they wanted. "No, nothing happened."

"How do you explain that?"

"I don't have to explain it. We were hiding at first, and

then my father and brother and I went to Zossen and got my mother, and then we got out of the Russian zone on a train."

Schwartz looked at a paper. "But your passport says that was not until August 1945."

"Yes."

He said, "But how did you survive in Berlin with all those soldiers around, communists, radicals?"

Anna knew what they wanted. Somehow they had information about her. For just a second she wondered if all the self-righteous and evil officials in the world worked for the same union, regardless of time or country. "I had a friend. An officer. A Soviet officer. He protected us."

The silence hung heavy. Let them dare to suggest any impropriety in that! They had been here during the war, safe from everything. Let them judge anyone who survived the hell she had been through. Mikhail ran the ration stand in Bernhardstrasse. He followed her one day and bought her coffee and bread. He was a painter and poet. Almost as young as she was. At that point Anna was living in a back room of Frau Dold's apartment in Zehlendorf with five other people and a thousand lice. Squatting in the corner of the yard that had become the toilet, her guts racked with dysentery. Her brother and father were sleeping in the forest at Zeuthener See, hiding from the soldiers, making their way to Zossen. One night Mikhail came to the apartment and told her that he was being transferred. He gave her a pass and a ticket for the train, and she was at her mother's house when her father and brother arrived.

CHAPTER FOUR
April 1947

Morton

MORT'S PLAN WAS to have his driver take Pamela back to the hotel after work so she could unwind and refresh. He would go over to the office and work for two hours, then come back so they could go for dinner. Then back to the hotel to make love, and back to the office by nine at the latest.

This plan began to fall apart immediately. When Henry called "Wrap!" someone opened the door of the soundstage and it was raining—a nice, heavy California spring shower through the slanting afternoon sunlight. So everyone just stood there, assuming it would stop in a few minutes. Then Henry broke out a bottle, his assistant found paper cups and ice, and suddenly it was a party for cast and crew. With the clock ticking, Mort decided to stay and then take her to the hotel himself and just do her there, without all the other stuff. She could order in after he left.

When the rain let up after about forty-five minutes, everyone ran out. Mort's driver was sitting by the open door, smoking, but not drinking, of course. "That'll be all for the night, Lin." Mort whacked him softly on the shoulder. "I'll drive myself."

"Alright. You sure?" Mort had had a drink, and the driver was concerned. That was a benefit of having a driver/watcher/keeper/protector. He'd hired Lin after the robbery, and had quickly come to rely on him, even if all he was doing was going to a perfectly safe tavern for a couple of pops. It was great to not have to worry about driving, in any condition. But he did not like to have Lin drive him to Pamela's hotel when he was going there to screw her. Just one more witness.

He whispered his plan to Pamela, and she left the studio and waited at the hot dog stand on Ince Boulevard, around a corner and up a block from the studio gate. Their usual rendezvous when he was taking her home. As Mort drove he described a new scene he was writing. Pamela sat next to him, listening quietly, content to be with him. Then, as Mort pulled up to the hotel—

"Oh God."

Mort had to wait until he finished turning into the parking space before he could look to see what Pamela was reacting to. He followed her eyes. An athletic young man with curly brown hair walked toward them. "That's—"

"Yeah."

Mort shut off the car. "When did he get—"

Pamela was already climbing out. She stood in the open car door as her husband approached. Mort felt trapped and exposed. He wished for Lin had driven. He wished he hadn't come. Was this a confrontation that could be avoided? He got out of the car on his side.

"Hi, baby!" Ken Preston fanned his arms out to embrace Pamela. She hugged him, but her purse slid down her arm and became a cushion between them, and then pushed them apart. He chuckled. "How are you?"

"Fine. Fine." She hitched up the purse and hugged him again. "It's so nice to see you."

He laughed and made a face. "So *nice?*" He hugged her again and they kissed. "Yeah, it's nice!"

Pamela made a quarter turn and gestured in Mort's direction. "You remember Mr. Blackwell."

Ken's attitude changed abruptly from boyish warmth to

stiff formality. "Yes," he intoned. "Of course. How do you do you do, sir."

By now Mort understood that Ken's appearance was not a surprise to Pamela, though maybe its timing was. As he walked around the back of the car he attempted a touch of charm. "Skip the *sir*. Your wife is doing a fabulous—"

"Yes, she's fabulous." Ken dropped the pretense of politeness and turned his attention to her. "So let's go celebrate!"

"Sure, let's do." She glanced at Mort. "Mr. Blackwell had invited me to have dinner. Let's all go—"

Ken looked only at her. "I'm sure he'll understand."

Mort did understand—that he had been caught almost in *flagrante delicto*. Now he just wanted to get away with as little fuss as possible. Certainly not have dinner with them. But he couldn't just leave her there either.

"Looks like you already started," said Pamela. Mort realized the young man had been drinking. But so had Pamela. She was tipsy when they left the party, and affectionate. She knew where they were going and what for.

"Oh, no, not really." Kenny reached to embrace her. "Then we can go home."

Pamela stepped back. "Home?"

"I got my own hotel. I told you."

Her shoulders slumped. "Oh. Where is it?"

"Downtown. You know—I told you."

"Yes, I know, but . . . I'd have to move, and—"

"Not tonight," he wheedled. "And what is there to move anyway?"

"You could have just stayed here."

"Oh no, I'm not staying here!" Ken's tone changed instantly. "I know what's going on." His eyes fixed on Mort, just long enough. "Believe me. I'm not going to crawl into that bed."

"There's nothing going on, Ken." Now she was angry,

too. "You need to—"

Ken jabbed a finger towards Mort. "Then what's he doing here?"

"He just gave me a ride. It was raining. Just dinner."

Mort of course knew exactly how much that was a lie. All he had to do was hold her hand on the way to the car, kiss her forehead, breath her fragrance, and she knew.

"I'm giving you a chance, honey." Ken leaned closer to her. "I'll forgive and forget. We were apart for a long time. Okay. But I'm back now. And we're back together. But it has to start tonight."

"Try to understand. I'm exhausted. And I've got early call tomorrow, and lines to learn. I really need some time alone to . . ."

"But you're my wife!" Ken whispered angrily. "I'm your husband! And I have to schedule an audience with you?" He was weeping tearlessly. "He's taken you away, hasn't he!"

Pamela shook her head, and she was crying, too. "No, Ken, no."

"He's torn it up!" Ken slashed the air in front of him with clenched fists. He turned, and looked at Mort, and Mort instinctively prepared to either run or fight. But he did not move.

"I know all about it," Ken growled at Mort. "You and her. I'd have to be blind. And there's nothing I can do about it." His eyes lit up like he was doing a scene from the Corsican Brothers or something. "Or maybe . . . I've seen the articles, the little bits from your lackeys, the gossip columnists. Y'see, that's what you do when you're in a crap play in New York and your wife is on the other side of the country with another man. You read a lot of newspapers."

"Ken!" Pamela said.

"Oh, I know. What a great story you've worked up for this picture. The saintly, teenage, unknown actress playing the holy role. Yeah, great. It'd take about five seconds for me to blow that up. Your saint is a twenty-four-year-old married woman who's had an abortion. And she's sleeping with her boss to help her career. Beautiful."

Pamela, blocked by cars and the wall of the hotel and Ken from going anywhere else, got back in the car and slammed the door. Ken yanked the door open.

"Get the hell away from me!" Pamela screamed, and pulled the door back closed. "Can we please *go!*" That was obviously directed at Mort.

Ken stood facing Mort, panting like he'd just run a mile. Mort, one of the great hard-asses in Hollywood, a man to whom arguing was a way of life and a passion, and almost the air he breathed, said nothing. He turned and walked back around the car and opened the door. Pamela was staring straight ahead, her face crimson with anger. Mort looked at Ken one more time and came to a decision. He had so far discouraged Pamela from divorcing the guy, for both personal and public relations reasons. Mort had no intention of divorcing Irene, and wanted Pamela as a long-term mistress, at least for a few months, until *Angeline* had been released and had a good run in theaters. By then, he figured he'd be over her and she could do what she wanted in her personal life. But he had to get this guy out of the way for now. Maybe Mort could arrange a job for him in another play, in New York, a good one that he could not resist. A long-running play. Mort would buy out the house himself every night if he had to, to keep that play running. And maybe the guy would agree to a quiet divorce. If you can't hide the truth from someone, you can make it worth their while not to see it.

Lyman

FOR SEVENTEEN DAYS Lyman Wilbur lived in a very disagreeable hotel. Drying out was a process he had been through before, and this time the physical effects—though they had never been less than torturous—were worse than ever. He didn't have the shakes or see pink elephants, but he felt feverish and sweaty and could not sleep without pills, which were provided. The pills knocked him out for hours of anxious dreams and unrestful half-sleep, so that he awoke feeling groggy and abandoned. He would be intensely hungry, especially for starchy foods like rice and noodles, but soon after eating he would become nauseous and the fever would return.

The cycle felt endless—or more accurately, bottomless—and Lyman would swing into fits of silent rage at anyone who spoke to him or even appeared before him. This outward anger was, of course, just a manifestation of his self-disgust, but he was too sick and sad to actually deal with his failings. The only time he felt human for the first three or four days was when he was blaming someone else for some trivial offense.

He had no visitors except Dr. Rosenstone. Who would visit him? His dead wife's niece? His second cousin from Toronto? No one cared whether he recovered or stepped in front of a bus. His only acquaintances were his agent, his publisher, and a couple of fellow writers who wrote him kind but pointless letters from time to time.

"Maybe," suggested Dr. Rosenstone, "you could consider that *you* are an important person in your life." When Lyman scoffed at that idea, the doctor continued: "And maybe you could grant yourself the privilege of being cared about."

This strangely purposeful misreading of his life had the perverse effect of giving Lyman a little hope. Caring about himself, to Lyman, meant writing and reading and thinking with purpose. He couldn't write anything at that point, of course, and didn't have the patience to read anything heavier than a magazine. But he did think, and that made the days a little easier to endure. By the fourth or fifth day he felt better, and then he knew the real challenge began. That would be the challenge of getting through a day without drink, a day when he did not need a drink, but simply wanted one, simply missed the pleasant evening ritual of a gin and tonic, a glass of wine.

But he had been through this part before and knew how to do it. So he gave in to sleep at the slightest urge and began to talk to himself, to give those imaginary radio interviews and university seminars that passed the time and sharpened his wits. He would need to write something eventually, to become absorbed in it. That would help immensely. He began to think more deeply about themes and outlines for a new book. He didn't have characters in mind yet, but he knew they would appear when needed. After all, the characters were going to be movie people, and he worked at a movie studio. The characters would make themselves known soon enough.

When he started to write magazine stories back in 1933, Lyman typed everything. Then he would mark up the page with a red pencil and retype it. But since he had become ensconced in movies he had taken to writing in longhand on the yellow legal pads that were stacked in the supply cabinets. Then a studio typist would knock it out. He didn't have any paper at the sanitarium, except for a couple of sheets of stationary on the desk in his room. So getting some paper would be one of the first things to do. Since he had plenty of time to think, he plotted out the paper acquisition in detail.

Rosenstone's visits were lengthy sessions in which Lyman

was forced to recount tales from his youth: the absent father, the devoted but struggling mother, the gruff and demanding stepfather. Lyman was tempted to fabricate stories just to escape the self-examination. He actually spent some off-hours reconstructing Dreiser's *American Tragedy* in his mind, thinking to pass it off as his own past, but when Rosenstone sat in the sessions with him like a Jewish-Siamese Buddha, all-seeing, all-knowing, Lyman lost his nerve and meekly offered up prosaic insights about his childhood and youth.

Finally one day, the doctor offered a rare morsel of praise, and followed that up with words Lyman had been longing to hear.

"I think you're ready to move out of here. The next phase is daily sessions, individual and group, and you can live at my residence."

Lyman already knew that by residence the doctor was referring to his clinic or sanitarium. He wondered if it would resemble Van Helsing's gothic asylum in *Dracula*, and if he would be watched over by a little man in a white suit with a Cockney accent and a push-broom mustache. But this was progress.

The car that showed up the next afternoon, Friday, was driven by a rough-looking, pink-cheeked man with a disinclination to converse. The place they arrived at was a sort of stucco Spanish castle set fairly close to the street, but with ample space to either side. Neighboring houses could be glimpsed through eucalyptus and orange trees. Lyman was taken to a guest house in the back that stood akimbo to a swimming pool and a large patio. In the evening he dined with the doctor in the spacious kitchen of the main house. Sitting in the kitchen rather than some sort of banquet room seemed like a homey touch, and Rosenstone was convivial and chatty, very unlike the therapist from their sessions.

"Relax tonight." Rosenstone sipped iced tea. "Tomorrow we'll get started."

The two of them seemed to be alone in the house, except for the cook who served them and disappeared into another room where she could be heard washing dishes and putting things in cupboards. After dinner Lyman returned to the cabana for the prescribed relaxation. It was a single room with a double bed and a sitting area composed of two comfortable chairs, a bookshelf and a small writing desk. The shelf contained bound copies of classics that seemed never to have been opened. If he was to spend any time here he would need to stock up on some decent reading matter.

And now was the time to start writing. He had a draft of his novel with him, and briefly considered going home to retrieve his portable typewriter. But he didn't feel ready to set foot in the home he had shared with Tina, which had scarcely been breathed in since the day she was taken to the hospital for the last time. A memory that still stabbed Lyman painfully but would not get him to take a drink.

So, legal pads.

CHAPTER FIVE
Friday, April 18

Priscilla

AS THEY WALKED past the cool grey and amber space of the lobby bar, Priscilla glanced at Mrs. B. "How about a couple of belts? After a day as a virgin I could use it. Not to mention that corset."

"Well . . ."

"I'm joking, I'm joking!" said Priscilla. "God knows." On her day off the previous Sunday, Priscilla had gone with some of her castmates to Long Beach, to the amusement park there, and had bought a cute little stuffed lion for Greggy, but she hadn't yet given it to Mrs. B. So this evening, Friday, Mrs. B. drove Priscilla to her hotel, and they were going up to her room now to fetch the gift.

When Priscilla opened the door of her room, she saw Ken sprawled on the sofa. She also saw a half-empty bottle of whiskey on the end table.

"'allo, 'allo!" he called brightly.

"How did you get in here?"

"How?" He levered himself upright. "I'm your husband. They gave me a key."

"I see." Priscilla was acutely conscious of Mrs. B. standing behind her, watching this.

"Well," he said. "Today's the day, you know. Are you ready to fall in love?"

"You smell like a saloon."

"Oh, not the whole saloon," Ken smiled. "Just this little bit." He picked up the pint bottle. "This little, oh, about . . ." He made measuring movements with his fingers. "About three inches of it." He unscrewed the cap and took a sip, then tipped the bottle toward Priscilla. "Ladies?"

Priscilla shook her head, furious with the hotel or the person working in it who had let him in, and furious at the idea that any man could waltz up and say he was her husband and they'd shrug and give him the key. Priscilla swung around him and set her purse on the small dinette table near the window.

"But I didn't mean fall in love with me," he said. "I meant the house."

"The house!"

"Today's the day, right? We agreed—"

"You promised you wouldn't do this."

"And you promised you *would* do this."

"And nothing has changed."

But something had changed. Priscilla had hired a lawyer who was going to draw up papers for a divorce. She had thought they would be delivered to Ken this week, but he hadn't yet mentioned receiving them. If he had not, Priscilla was glad. She did not want a personal confrontation. That's why you hire a lawyer, and why your hotel doesn't let people into your room that you don't want to see.

"It's been a week!" he pouted.

On the other hand, maybe he had got the papers, and this was his response—to pretend it hadn't happened and try to talk her back into a marriage. Priscilla had never heard of someone doing that. Which didn't mean Kenny wouldn't try. "No," she said. "Today is not the day." She turned toward Mrs. Brown. "Sorry about all this. I appreciate—"

"Look," Ken interrupted. "I've had it!" The boozy humor was gone. "We're going to go out there. You can drive."

Priscilla turned to him and planted her feet. "No!"

Everything about who Priscilla was and where she was from, and her whole history with Ken, fought against what she was doing. But everything about who she had become and where she wanted to go told her it was the right thing to do. There comes a point. You never wish it, but when it comes you face it.

Mrs. B., who had not moved at all, turned and closed the door behind her, and Priscilla realized she had shouted. But it was too late to worry about that, or to try to hide anything from Mrs. B.

"We'll be apart no longer," said Ken. He made a chopping motion with his hand. "This ends today."

Priscilla pulled a cigarette from her bag and lit it. Over her shoulder she said. "No. I need more time."

"More time?" His voice rose. "It's been four months since you left. Actually almost six already!" She could hear the hurt and humiliation in his voice. That was real. But he was also an actor, and you always had to keep that in mind.

"I don't care how long it's been." She looked at him. "You've been acting very, you know, strange since you got here. Demanding this and demanding that. I almost feel like I don't know you anymore. And I almost wonder if I ever did."

He jumped up and stood swaying, his eyes burning into her. "Oh, great, just great!"

"Okay, you have to calm down now, you have to stop shouting."

Mrs. B. stepped forward. "Okay kids. Neutral corners. Why don't we all sit down and get some things ironed out?"

She motioned to Ken to return to the sofa, and to Priscilla to sit in the club chair facing Ken, but out of his reach. Grateful for someone else to deflect him, Priscilla crushed out her cigarette and sat down. Ken returned to his seat within reach of the bottle. Mrs. B. took one of the dining chairs and placed it to form the third side of a square. Instead of sitting in it she stood behind it, leaning on stiff arms.

"Ken, do you know who I am?" she asked.

"Sure. Studio."

"Yeah, the studio. And I know who you are, too. You need to realize that your wife is involved with other men."

Priscilla's stomach fluttered with surprise. She cringed inwardly, afraid of the next thing she imagined was going to be said. She need not have worried.

Mrs. B. continued. "Men. With Mr. Norman, who wrote the book, Mr. Koehler, who is directing the picture, and Mr. Blackwell, who is producing."

Ken's face lit up with delight, and he guffawed. "Oh, lordy lord!"

"She is yelled at and wheedled at and begged for things all day long." Mrs. B. stepped around the chair and sat down, leaning toward Ken. "And being men, they all insist that she do what they want. And being a woman, she tries to give it to them. You're an actor. But you're also a man. It's different for a woman, especially on a film set, which is like a slow-motion war. Especially when you're having to deal with Mort Blackwell."

Ken had gradually sunk back into the couch. "Of course. Of course. But he's sleeping with my wife. Y'see?" He spoke in a sad, quavering voice. "I'd like to beat his ass, but I can't get at him."

He seemed emotionally and physically beaten, and Priscilla fought the urge to console him, to reassure him. To give in to him.

"Oh come on," Mrs. B. scoffed. "Let's be adults here. Your wife is doing important work, and it's going to make her an important person. She's a great actress and this is her chance. Do you want to deny her that? This is her dream."

Ken leaned back. "You're missin' the point." He let out a sigh of weary frustration. "I'm tired of argoon. Just tired."

"You've got to be a realist." Mrs. B. leaned toward him again. "Her career is about to take off, and yours isn't. That's

not easy for you. Not for any man who's worth a goddamn."
Mrs. B. sat back. "But this is where you earn it."

Ken stared at her, a little dazed at her forthright approach. Or maybe from the drink. "Earn what?"

"It." She held an invisible ball in front of her and shook it. "*It*. The thing you want, the thing she wants, we all want. It takes patience and humility. That's what she needs from you. Can you give her that?"

But he had been tipping slowly over, and now stared vacantly at the arm of the sofa, listening to music only he could hear. His anger spent and even his awareness slipping away. Priscilla had never seen this kind of behavior, this wild swing from passionate anger to a kind of torpor.

As she stared at him, in a turmoil of thoughts, guilt, and memories, she thought of a particular afternoon in New York—had it only been last year? Walking down by the Chelsea piers, a cool, sunny day, laughing, their joy as big as the clear blue sky, knowing the great things they would do together. And now this.

Mrs. B. went over to the room phone on the nightstand and picked it up. Soon she was having a conversation Priscilla only half heard. Ken seemed to have passed out. Priscilla stood and went to the window and stared out, still in New York, that sunny day.

Mrs. B. was beside her. "You've been seeing Dr. Rosenstone, I think you told me."

Priscilla wondered if he would be coming over. "Yes, I have."

She nodded. You've been to his clinic? You know he has rooms there?"

"Yes."

"Good, good. A car is coming to take you there." Mrs. B. nodded toward Ken, leaning over the arm of the couch. "I've got to get him out of here, but he won't go if you are here."

Priscilla was grateful for someone taking charge. "That's

a good idea. A girl from our group stayed there. It's like, a refuge."

"Exactly," said Mrs. B. "You go there tonight. I'll see that Ken gets home and gets tucked in. So you go to the doctor's place, take the weekend off, and I'll call you there."

"But the shooting tomorrow."

"That's been cancelled. You're on vacation as of now. At least for the weekend. Talk to Doc Rosenstone. Find your center of gravity. Relax. That'll be the best thing. Ken won't know where you are, Mort won't know. No one will bother you. I'll take care of it. Don't worry."

"But what about Ken?"

"Don't worry about him, take care of yourself."

Morton

MORTON BLACKWELL SAT back in his chair, holding the microphone of a dictating machine in his left hand and picking through a jumble of handwritten notes that lay on the desk.

He clicked the record button on the microphone. "And it goes without saying that the lighting of Miss Lindgren is as crucial as the photography, the makeup, or her own natural beauty."

He released the button and picked up another piece of paper. He resumed speaking into the microphone. "And as to makeup, I want it understood that her eyebrows are not to be plucked without my approval. Or in fact my being present. And in keeping with the effort to give Miss Lindgren an utterly natural look, at no time is her eyeshadow to be darker than MF 22 without my personal approval."

He set down the microphone and picked up a different one attached to another dictating machine that stood on a rolling rack next to the desk. He stared for a moment at the blackness of the dark window across from where he sat. This night work all had to do with the studio's other assets. He was spending most of his days arranging the financing and release of *Angeline*. Not to mention rewriting the script.

"New memo, draft only. Mr. Wyler being unable to implement the requirements of this picture he is hereby terminated as director, per the terms of his contract with Morton Blackwell Productions. Mrs. Brown, please type this yourself and bring it for my final decision. Strictly confidential, of course."

The light on Blackwell's phone blinked. He released the record button on the Dictaphone. Mrs. Brown had left at six per usual. That was the way Mort wanted it. "No," he had told her when he had established this policy. "You're a mother. You should have a home life, even if I don't." It was understood by both of them that his office at the studio was more Mort's home than any house he had ever lived in.

"Yes," Mrs. Brown had said. "I appreciate that. But if you ever need me to—"

"Sure, sure. But it's more important that you are here on time in the morning, ready to roll."

She chuckled and mimicked typing with both hands. Even though she was much more than a secretary, the first job, first thing every morning, was to oversee the typing and distributing of the memos Mort had dictated into the machines the previous evening. There would usually be dozens of these memos, and they could be long. Birdie from the clerical pool came to pick up the recording cylinders from one machine, and Mrs. Brown kept the ones from the second machine, which she would type herself. Those were the confidential ones that Blackwell would review and revise or just rip up—the ones in which employees got fired, deals were made or killed, important people were begged for forgiveness or more time or more money.

Mort stared at the silently blinking light of the telephone. After six in the evening only those who knew his direct line could call him. That would be maybe a dozen people. Of those dozen, there was really only one he wanted to hear from. He picked up the receiver. "Mort here."

"Hi, it's—"

"Pam! How are you, darling?"

"Hi. Oh, fine, I guess. But remember, it's always Pamela, not Pam. That was your order."

"You're right!" Mort was pleased she remembered. "So, Pamela, how'd it go today?"

"Oh, okay."

"Couldn't get down there."

"No, it was fine."

Mort sensed something amiss. "You getting along with Henry?"

"Oh, most certainly."

The line went silent while Mort waited for her to finish the thought. But maybe she had.

"Mrs. Brown called to tell me you needed to take the day off. Are you feeling alright?"

"No."

Again a portentous silence.

"Well, it's not a problem. I'm sure they can work around you tomorrow anyway. And I still don't like your dress in the castle scene. The historian tells me it's authentic, but it's boring. You're supposed to be an Italian countess, not a chess piece." Mort stopped, conscious that he was not hearing agreement, demurrer or even acknowledgement. "Is there something you want to say to me?"

He heard a long breath. "No."

"Well, maybe I'll come by on the way home?"

"No," said Pamela. "You better not. I'm going to bed, and I might have a cold coming on. I just don't think—"

"Sure, I understand." But he didn't understand what was going on with her and feared it might involve her husband, might involve losing her. Mrs. Brown hadn't mentioned the husband when she called, but Mort knew he was out there and a threat in several ways.

He thought of a topic. "Oh, by the way, I'm reading *Forever Amber*. I think it's perfect for your next one. You've been wanting me to read it. And now I see why."

"Good. I think it's a great story." At last a glimmer of enthusiasm. She was always interested in her career.

"The woman who rises from the gutter to the . . . whatever? She rises. And the English start drinking tea instead of coffee."

"Oh, yes. I remember."

Her weary sigh came over the phone, and Mort saw her face before him, her sweet lips creased into a smile, her dark eyes shining. He longed to be with her. But it was no good. "Alright, I'll let you go."

"Alright. Good night."

Mort hung up the phone, worried and frustrated. Why would she call, and then say nothing? What was the message he was not getting? Normally, he wouldn't let a frail get under his skin. And he wondered if she had. He had become very ambivalent about her. Eager to move on, but also jealous and possessive.

In his marriage to Elaine, he had been a serial adulterer, a hopeless gambler and sometime boozer. Now he wondered if he was having the schoolboy crush he'd never had time for as an actual schoolboy. Part of it was that virginal appeal she had, even though she was married to another man. That man, Mort was certain, did not see in her what he saw: an impossible mixture of raw animal beauty and unworldly grace. When he had finally seduced her, he had been slow and patient, the way a romantic woman imagines the act of love.

Mort sighed and clicked the button on the microphone. "Another draft, confidential, Mrs. Brown. Have you found anything for Ken Preston in New York? He is a theatre actor, so that would be ideal. We should look for a long-term project for him. I haven't heard from Myron Seitz for awhile. Get ahold of him."

Yes, it would be highly desirable for the husband to return to New York. At least for a few more months. By fall, Mort felt sure, he would be over his infatuation with Pamela. Then the husband could do what he wanted.

That was the plan. If he did not get over her, his life would certainly get more complicated. So he would get over her.

There was a soft knock on the office door.

Anna

ANNA KEPT ON with her speech lessons, auditioned as a singer (very good) and as a dancer (not so). She read for parts, tested costumes and hairstyles. She continued to receive pressure about her name, and to be questioned about her background. One day she would be asked if she was sure she wasn't German, the next day if she was sure she wasn't Polish, Austrian, Swedish ("you look Swedish") or Hungarian.

She was called in for rehearsals for a picture about the last days of the war. She thought, if I can't play that, I'll just go home and forget about it. The day was spent in rehearsal, blocking out scenes and camera and lighting positions. She went home expecting to be called back, but nothing happened. She called her agent, Siegel, and he said he would look into it.

A few days later she had just sat down to dinner with Ferdie when the phone rang.

Ferdie answered. "This is her husband. Yes. Alright." He handed her the phone. "The office."

The woman on the phone said, "Mister Blackwell would like to see you at ten."

"Tomorrow morning?"

"Tonight."

Anna was told how to get to the executive offices, which were located several blocks from the studio lot she had been going to. She was assured that the security guards would help her find her way once she arrived. So she finished dinner, washed her face, redid her makeup and put on the blue day dress with the fitted bodice that buttoned all the way to the collarbone. And she took her half-length gloves in the complementary strawberry pink.

Ferdie drove her through sleepy streets to the office. He said he would wait in the car. The two young guards, one tall and swarthy, the other chubby and soft, directed her down the main hall to Blackwell's suite. "No one will be in the outer office," said the dark one. "Just knock on the door. The double door right in the middle."

She followed these instructions and walked through the deserted building, which was richly decorated and furnished, at least compared to the warehouses and cottages that made up most of the studio facilities. She found the office and the double doors, and knocked with two gloved fingers. A voice inside told her to enter. She went in through the right-hand door and closed it behind her.

Morton Blackwell sat behind a large desk, speaking on the phone. He motioned her to come in, and indicated a sitting area near a fireplace, where a fire burned steadily and somewhat incongruently. It was not a very cool evening outside, and the fire was a little too warm to be comfortable. Nevertheless, Anna did as instructed and sat on the couch, as far away as she could from the fire.

Blackwell kept talking, finishing one call and starting another, murmuring in a low voice with an occasional chuckle, or loudly making a point. Anna sat, not listening. After a while she realized that the fireplace was really a gas grate, whose blue and gold flames curled around the birch logs without burning them. So they must be made of stone or concrete, or iron perhaps.

The words Blackwell said into the phone meant nothing to her. "She's such a goddam bitch . . . I want him gone and I don't care how . . . they can go fuck themselves . . . no, red, red! Crimson isn't red! . . . up to Catalina for the week-end . . . "

Ever since she had arrived in California Anna had felt uncomfortably out of place, being inspected, poked and posed. She had a sense of unreality, of disorientation. America was strange; California was strange; and Hollywood strangest of all, at least to judge by her very limited experience here.

She sat and gazed at the steady flame licking at the concrete logs. The producer kept talking, one phone call after another. An hour passed. Anna wondered about Ferdie, sitting all this time in the parking lot. After another ten minutes, she looked at her watch and became aware that the voice had stopped talking, and that Blackwell was moving to a bar against the wall and then toward her. He held two glasses half filled with a dark liquid.

He sat in the chair diagonal to hers, placing the drinks on the low table before them. He stretched upward and softly groaned, rolling his head around and trying to loosen his neck, like someone just released from a long confinement. The gas fire flared briefly, and his glasses glinted in the light. His expensive suit was rumpled and creased, as if he had been wearing it for days.

He picked up one of the glasses and took a deep swig. "Tell me everything about yourself."

This was the first time Anna had really talked to him. He had breezed into the room during the formal contract signing to welcome her to Hollywood. As if, she thought at the time, he was Hollywood and Hollywood was he. Then he'd breezed right back out again.

Now she felt intimidated by the command to recite— remembering her encounter with the disbelieving publicity fellow. This was the man who would control her career, her opportunities, her fate. What if her accent put him off, or she made dumb grammatical errors in English? What if he thought her stupid, or too foreign, or too difficult to understand?

All this tension and weight made for a terrible case of stage fright. But she called on her training and pushed through. She spoke mostly about her career, what she'd learned about acting and theatre—" . . . and Max Reinhardt, who had such an influence, Witkiewicz—do you know of him? Such chaos in Poland in the last ten years, but a great theatrical tradition—" and of the four films she'd made in Berlin, and the one in France that had not been released. She said as little as possible about her life in Berlin, or her personal journey since then. After her visit to the Jewish Committee, she was simply not going to discuss that anymore.

Blackwell sat taking notes on one of the thin, flat writing pads that seemed ubiquitous in this studio. When she came to a good stopping place, she stopped.

"An interesting story in itself." Blackwell said. He rose and walked back to the desk, where he dropped his pad and pen. He went to a door opposite the sitting area and opened it. Anna saw white tile and a sink. He went in and closed the door, and soon she heard water running. Was he taking a shower?

Now her discomfort doubled. Had she been dismissed? Forgotten about? This was an important man who moved from topic to topic and task to task without notice. The shower shut off, and she had decided definitely to leave when the door opened and Blackwell emerged. The rumpled jacket and the tie were gone, and the untucked white shirt looked fresh. His hair glistened, and damp feathers of it curled around his large, smooth, pale forehead. He walked up and stood directly before her in the wavering light of the fire. He extended his hand and she took it and rose to her feet, somewhat trapped between him and the couch.

"You're an interesting girl. And beautiful." He smiled, and stood there as if waiting, reeking of mouthwash and aftershave. "I like you. I would like to know you better. Would you like to get to know me?"

Anna, completely at a loss, stammered a response that

seemed idiotic even as she said it. "Yes, I, of course, I would always welcome—"

"That could be arranged." He moved even closer. The little spikes of damp hair waggled above her as his air of menacing authority broke for the first time into a real smile. But in that smile Anna saw the assurance of absolute power that she had seen in German politicians before the war, in Russian officers as they strode through the rubbled bricks of destroyed Berlin. He reached up to her throat, hooked the opening of her dress and pulled roughly down, tearing it open. Buttons flew in the air and disappeared in the darkness at her feet.

Anna pushed him away and moved as quickly as she could to the bathroom, her stomach heaving. She barely had time to lock the door before she could lean over the sink and vomit. She sagged on shaky legs, elbows on the cold tile of the counter, and vomited again. Then she sank to the floor gasping. She had no thoughts, only an overpowering fear of what was on the other side of that door. She expected it to crash open at any moment.

Her stomach trembled again but held, and after several long minutes, she began to think about how to save herself. She pushed herself up and looked in the mirror, checking her dress. Some of the buttons had not ripped off, enough that it could be closed in a more or less seemly fashion, if Ferdie did not look too closely.

She checked her face, patted her hair with trembling hands, smoothed the front of the dress. She had to get out of here, even if it meant—the mouthwash! There stood the bottle on the counter, next to a stack of small paper cups. She would throw it in his face when he approached her. That would give her a few seconds to get to the door. She filled one of the cups halfway and leaned close to the door to listen. The low voice, as before. He was back on the phone!

She pushed the door open and walked quickly toward the

double doors, holding the cup of mouthwash in one hand, grabbing her bag and gloves with the other. She grasped the doorknob, but it wouldn't turn, and the door was stuck. She heaved a breath of frustration.

He called out loudly, so she would know he was talking to her. "You've got a screen test at Colosseum. Mrs. Brown will call you with the details."

Anna stared at the door, only vaguely aware of the words. She pulled on the knob again. There was a buzz behind the door somewhere, and it clicked and opened. So it had been locked. She shuddered.

Stepping out to the waiting room she pulled the door firmly closed. There was a large multiline phone on the receptionist's desk there, with one yellow light lit. Anna held the cup over the phone and poured the mouthwash out in a slow stream over the dialer and the buttons, finding every little crevice. The light went out. Anna dropped the paper cup on the floor, and found her way down the hall, back past the sullen guards, who sit here every night. They would know. They would have to.

Ferdie was slouched in the corner of the front seat. She opened the passenger door and slid in. There was no way she could tell him about this, at least not now. It would take an iron will just to get through the rest of the evening until she could lie in bed and give in to her emotions.

He roused himself. "So what happened?"

She stared straight ahead. "Nothing."

He shrugged and pushed the starter. "Are they changing your name?"

"Yes. Kochanka."

Ferdie stared at her. "What?"

"Let's just go."

"Okay, okay, we're going."

And he drove home mystified, since he didn't know a word of Polish.

CHAPTER SIX
Saturday, April 19

Dr. Rosenstone

THE PHONE ON Rosenstone's nightstand rang, and before he was fully conscious of his actions, he rolled toward it and reached out to the sound. Middle-of-the-night calls were always tiring and frustrating. His primary personal goal for any patient was that that they become strong enough to never call him at . . . 12:25 in the morning, his bedside clock said.

He pulled himself up a little and put the receiver to his ear. "Hello."

"Doctor?" Male voice.

"Yes."

"This's Joe. Gianelli. I'm your patient. Or I used to—there's a problem. He's dead." There was a burst of static.

"Yes, I remember you, Joe. Now who are you talking about?"

"Kenny Preston. Isn't he a patient of yours?"

Rosenstone sat up and made a determined swim to full consciousness. "No. Priscilla—"

"It's her husband."

"And he's—"

"Dead." The voice broke a little.

"God! Are you sure?"

"I need someone to come here," said the voice. "Can you come over?"

Of course he would go. Priscilla was his patient, and Ken was one of her problems, mainly as a source of guilt. She had been untrue to him, had possibly aborted the child he wanted, and she worried that he would not be able to handle her success. For those and other reasons he thought he better get his ass out there. The address was off Hyperion up toward Glendale, not that far. He dressed quickly and drove through the dark streets with a cold stone behind his ribs and an irrational hope that Joe was wrong.

But Joe was right. Ken Preston lay slumped against a wall in the living room of a barely furnished house. He was fully dressed in slacks and a sport coat, and it appeared he had just keeled over and gone to sleep. No sign of violence or struggle or great pain.

"Were you here?"

"No, he called me. About eleven thirty, I guess. I could tell he was loaded. He's been dealing with, well, you know. I tried to tell him to just hit the sheets and sleep it off. But he wasn't making sense. He said he was burning his furniture. That sounded bizarre, so I came over. I got here just before I called you."

Rosenstone realized he had been aware of a slight acrid stench since he walked into the house. In a fireplace in the far wall of the mostly empty room, something was smoldering, making a lot of white smoke.

"When I got here, he was just lying on the floor. I pulled him up, and shook him. I tried to wake him up. I don't know if he was still alive or not. I thought he moved, y'know, I thought he made a sound. Then I went into the kitchen to get some water, splash him, you know? When I came back, he was—" Joe flipped his hand toward the inert form. "I shook him, I slapped him. Just nothing."

Rosenstone kneeled beside the young man, wondering for the thousandth time at how people could hate themselves, or hate life, so much. This had been a poor confused kid. Now that was all he ever would be.

Priscilla had come to Rosenstone on a referral from someone in Morton Blackwell's office. That would not have been unusual. He had treated Elaine Blackwell for several years, and even had a few months of sessions with the great man himself. That had not gone well. Blackwell was argumentative and intransigent, and obviously believed that he understood his own mind, and maybe the entire field of psychiatry, better than his doctor. But he had turned out to be a valuable source of referrals.

Priscilla Preston, on the other hand, had been a willing and enthusiastic analysand. She and her husband had been exposed to psychoanalysis in New York. She was just deeply, almost cripplingly neurotic, but Ken, from what she told Rosenstone, was a classic manic-depressive, and possibly already drug dependent. Rosenstone was very strict about the use of sleeping pills and so-called tranquilizers. He both doubted the efficacy and knew they could be dangerously addictive and easy to overdose. Which is what he assumed had happened here. Yes, there was the smell of alcohol, but for young, healthy people, drinking to the point of alcohol poisoning was almost unheard of.

He stood up and looked around. Through the dining alcove, he could see a bit of the kitchen, and a phone on the counter. He knew that Priscilla had another doctor, Rosenstone's friend Gene Garman, and assumed that he might also be Ken's GP. If this was an overdose, Garman's name could be on the prescription. He would need to know. Rosenstone walked into the kitchen and picked up the phone.

Joe trailed after him. "That phone was just put in a day or two ago." His voice quavered. "It maybe was only used three times. All tonight."

Now Rosenstone remembered that Joe was a writer. That's the way a writer thinks–the tragedy of the phone, just installed, never to be used again. That was a writer finding a punchline. It added a wrinkle, because Joe was a reporter or a columnist for the *Hollywood Reporter* or the *Star*, and boy, had he stumbled onto a story. Or had he? There was a dead man here, and a live one telling a story. Rosenstone had come to this house as a doctor, out of concern for a patient, and a tragic young man. Now he had a strong sense of possible danger and intrigue he might be drawn into.

When Garman arrived, he looked Ken over carefully and pointed out a film of clear, liquid vomit on the carpet where the young man had slumped over. Garman called the police, and sent Joe outside to wave them in.

Rosenstone went into the bedroom, where a pillow and a full ashtray sat in the corner, and a cheap cardboard trunk with a leather valise standing on top formed an island in the center of the room. He went into the bathroom. There on the counter he found two bottles of pills from a Glendale drugstore, identical except that one was empty. He did not recognize the name of the drug, but certainly knew the name of the prescribing physician: Dr. Kness. He put the full bottle in his pocket and went back to the kitchen. By the phone lay a datebook with a leatherette cover. Rosenstone picked it up and it opened in the middle, where several slips of paper had been stuffed: a receipt from a men's store and an uncashed check for ten dollars made out to A & P. The police were now coming up the walk. He could hear Joe's voice giving them his description of events.

Lyman

IN THE MORNING it became evident that the compound was not deserted. While still in bed Lyman heard muted tones of a conversation that seemed to be coming from the patio. And a gardener raking or hoeing with determination somewhere.

He lay drowsing in bed until after ten, when that urgent hunger overtook him. He rose and dressed in the same clothes he had worn the day before, and his last pair of clean socks.

By now silence had returned to the surroundings, and he stepped out into a sunny late morning. The doctor had told him that he could get breakfast and lunch in the kitchen, though no particular times were mentioned. As he stood there squinting in the bright light, nothing looked familiar; he could not recall how he had navigated the route the previous evening. And across the plaza-sized patio, a woman was watching him.

She lay on a chaise lounge in the shade of the house, looking like a coed in a pleated skirt and collared blouse with a green and yellow scarf spilling out of the neckline. Lyman had no idea who she might be, other than not a cook or a maid. Was Rosenstone married? The girl looked young enough to be the man's daughter. Which meant nothing, of course. The good doctor could obviously afford a harem of wives or a boarding school of daughters.

She lifted her hand as he approached, and gave him a shy smile.

"Hello," said Lyman.

"Hi."

"I'm new here. My name is Lyman."

"I'm Priscilla." She pointed in the direction from which

Lyman had come. "I'm your neighbor."

Lyman turned and looked back, and only then realized that the walkway split, and went to two doors set in identical halves of a duplex, of which he had the nearer half. "Oh!" he said lamely. "I see."

"A fellow inmate." The acerbic comment was contradicted by her utterly open and innocent expression.

It was hard for Lyman to believe that she was there for the same reason he was. "Are you a patient of Doctor Rosenstone's?"

"Oh, yes. He's been a godsend for me."

Again that simple sincerity, and Lyman realized that he was talking to an actress. "That's good to hear. Um, are you doing sessions? He mentioned that there might be some sort of sessions with other, uh, patients?" Lyman felt bashful talking even elliptically about someone else's mental condition. Especially with this pretty young woman, who seemed to glow with a sort of placid healthfulness.

"Oh, the group!" She nodded. "You'll enjoy the group. It might seem intimidating at first, but the people in it are, well, interesting. And it's great to get—to realize—that one's problems aren't actually unique, or maybe so terrible. But I don't think I'll be doing the group. Can you keep a secret?"

"I can try."

"I'm taking a break from my husband. We've been having problems. Doc Robby offered this, and I took it. It's really an escape."

"I see." Lyman looked around, appraising the level of privacy the place afforded. He had not been in real estate for nearly twenty years, but he could still size up a property. The area behind the house he judged to be something less than an acre, maybe one hundred and fifty feet wide across the back of the house, the pool, the patio and the cottages. The English garden, or park, rolled slightly uphill from the house etcetera about sixty or seventy yards, ending in a row of towering eucalyptus trees at the top of the rise. Stucco walls near the house gave way to a thick, tall hedge of some kind farther out. All in all, it was secure enough to make Lyman wonder if the purpose was to keep intruders out or the residents in.

"Well," he said. "It's quite a hideout."

"Absolutely." Her tone suggested contentment.

"So I am actually looking for the kitchen. I arrived late, and . . . would you happen to—"

The woman pointed over her left shoulder. "That door."

Lyman oriented himself. "I see. Thank you, uh—"

"Priscilla."

"Thanks, Priscilla." It seemed rude to leave her there. "Mm, do you want something?"

She laughed brightly. "What a funny thing to ask a rabbit. Oh, you mean to eat. No, I—"

"No, please," Though confused by her words, Lyman tried to match her jolly tone. "Show me where the kitchen is, and I'll buy you a cup of coffee, if they have it."

She smiled and tilted her head in a sort of acquiescence. Her arm reached toward him, and he took her hand as she rose. He hoped she saw his request as he intended it, which was friendly but not pushy. He just did not want to enter that house alone. Dr. Rosenstone might be his only hope of salvation, but Lyman did not want to interrupt or surprise or bump into him, or anyone, as he wandered into strange rooms. And Priscilla seemed to know him well enough. "Doc Robbie," and all that. Lyman was sure he would never get that comfortable with a psychiatrist.

She led him through the door into the kitchen. The same cook as last night stood facing the counter, involved with a purple vegetable that Lyman did not recognize.

"Yes sir?" asked the cook over her shoulder.

"Do you have coffee?"

"Yes sir, right there." She pointed to a small version of a

restaurant coffee machine, white porcelain cups arranged beside it. "If you wouldn't mind helping yourself."

Lyman waited a tic, no more, to see if the young woman beside him would move to pour the coffee. But she did not. Lyman stepped around her to the counter, overturned two cups and filled one with the steaming hot coffee. He looked at her and she nodded. He filled the second cup and returned the pot to its warmer.

"There's sugar and milk on the table," said the cook.

They sat across from one another at one end of the rectangular table in the middle of the room.

"So, Priscilla, to coin a phrase, are you in pictures?"

She gave him a wary look, then smiled. "Of course. You?"

"Well, technically. I'm really in words." He had confused her. "I'm a writer. And you're an actress, of course."

"Of course? Why couldn't I be a writer?"

"You're too obviously intelligent. I didn't say I was a great writer. The evidence suggests that for the most part, I'm not even a good one. What have you been in?"

"Nothing important."

Now that they were indoors, he could see her more clearly. She was certainly pretty enough to be in movies, with a sweet expression, like a Joan Bennett or Beverly Lloyd. "Give me a title."

She blushed. "I'm just starting out. It's called *Angeline*. We're finishing up shooting soon. I hope."

The title meant nothing to Lyman, and the woman's lack of enthusiasm led him to believe it was just a programmer. More hamburger from a studio meat grinder. "So how is it going?"

"I think it's alright. I don't know how to judge that. I've seen some of it. But I don't like watching myself."

Lyman sipped coffee. Priscilla stirred hers slowly and carefully, not clanking the spoon against the cup.

"You mentioned a rabbit," he said.

She propped an elbow on the table and rested her chin in a small, white hand. "Oh, that's me. I'm a rabbit. Foxes and weasels and, oh, you know, birds and snakes want to eat me up. At least that's how I feel. I told you I was hiding from my husband. I'm also hiding from my boss. He thinks he's in love with me."

"Your boss?"

"The head of the studio. He's my producer. Also my agent, my manager, my dentist."

"Dentist?"

"He might as well be. He controls everything else. Why not my teeth?"

She laughed softly, and Lyman could feel the emptiness of it.

He said, "I could see where that sort of thing might start to wear."

"He also changed my name. To Pamela Carr. Do you like it?"

"Versus Priscilla?" Lyman shrugged. "Hard to say."

She smiled appreciatively. "I'm still getting used to it." Maybe an actress, but also a human being. She had stopped stirring the coffee but still hadn't tasted it. "But enough about me," she said. "You just heard more of the truth about me than I spill in a year. Why are you here? Failed attempt? Guilt? Or guilt about a failed attempt?"

Lyman was a little nonplussed at these rapid shifts in tone. Who was he really talking to here? "I'm a drunk, he said. "I'm taking the waters."

"The what?"

Lyman forced himself to stop being sardonic. "You have been in these group sessions?"

"Yes. Some people really find them helpful. To be able to talk to someone who's been there, and yet you don't feel like you're just complaining. It breaks down that feeling of isolation."

"I don't know. My isolation, I think, is about all I have left that's really mine."

She smiled.

"But you're not participating?" he said.

"Yes, I'm in a group on Tuesdays. I recommend trying it. They have several different ones."

Lyman was still dubious about being trapped in a herd of neurotics. "I don't know."

"You know who gets the most out of the group?"

"Who?"

"The drinkers. They support one another, remarkably so."

"Well, I've lost my supporters. Now I only have keepers." Lyman cringed inwardly at the hollowness of his alleged wit.

"No." She reached across the table and laid her hand on Lyman's. "No, that's the past. We'll be friends. We'll concentrate on the future. What do you say?"

Anna

THE FIRST THING Anna thought about when she opened her eyes in the morning was the damp petals of dark hair that had wobbled slightly when Blackwell loomed over her and ripped her dress open. And the cold predator look in his eyes. The next thing she thought of was Ferdie, who thank God had already gone when she awoke. She knew he would have an intense reaction, but she did not know what it would be or how she should respond to it, and him.

Soft sunlight was coming through the drapes. She looked around the little bedroom and felt very alone.

Ferdie was everything that Morton Blackwell seemed was not. Honorable, with inner strength and integrity. They met in Frankfurt, where Anna and her family got off the train. Now in the U.S. zone, they had to report to officials who wanted to keep track of people but had little help to offer. This dilemma, of course, reminded Anna of Mikhail, her Red Army benefactor in Berlin.

By the rules of the occupation, U.S. personnel were forbidden to meet or talk to Germans. It was called fraternization, a brotherly-sounding term that did not at all apply to most of the contact that was going on. German women who went with the soldiers were ostracized, to the extent that starving and homeless people can shame anyone.

Ferdie was at the office where she went to apply for a passport. All that was in the hands of the Americans, partly because the German government had ceased to exist. With a passport one could at least begin the process of applying for a visa to come to the U.S. This had become the dream and obsession of her family, particularly her father, who blamed himself for not getting out of Germany in '36, when it would have been easier.

Ferdie was there mainly because he spoke a rough but

practicable German. He was from a farm town in Illinois where a large community of Westphalian immigrants had been living since the 1870s. He had just completed his degree in mechanical engineering when he was drafted, but ended up in the public affairs division, writing draft memos for superiors. When she met him she was suffering from constant hunger, lice, and dysentery. The last thing she had eaten was a half a loaf of stale bread and some wilted cabbage, which she split with her brother.

He had helped her that day. She was a virgin when they married, a fact that surprised him, as he was suffering from a delusion that all European girls engaged in intercourse.

✧   ✧   ✧

NOW SHE WAS faced with a decision. On her way out the door Blackwell had shouted a job at her. Was that how he bought her off? Was that how he apologized? To do anything that he told her to do, or take anything he gave her, would be to forgive what he did. How could she do that? Since the moment he attacked her, the world had become a frozen place, and Anna was frozen in it. She could see neither left nor right, neither forward nor back.

And she was suddenly drained of ambition, trapped in a nightmare. Under contract to Blackwell. He determined her fate. So maybe she should accept this gift as an atonement. She really had no choice.

No! She would go home. She could get along there somehow. They were still on rations in France, Germany, everywhere, but she'd go back. But Ferdie couldn't leave. He had a career to think of. And now her career was over. So they would have to stay in what was now the last city in the world where Anna wanted to be.

She called Siegel, her agent. Not because she had an idea what she should do, or even a good idea what she would say to him, but just because she had to talk to someone.

Apparently Blackwell or someone had called him, because he already knew about the appointment.

"Wednesday," he said. "Colosseum Pictures. Nine a.m. Ask for Mr. Arlen, or Arline. Don't know who that is. Doesn't matter."

Anna listened without a word. After a few seconds of silence, Siegel said, "I know, I know. It's been tough." His voice softened. "But this is the business. You knock on doors till you knock 'em down."

"He tried to rape me." She was surprised how calm she sounded.

"Uh, what?"

"He tore my clothes. He put hands on me."

"Who did?"

"Blackwell. Last night."

"You were with Blackwell last night?"

"Yes, for a meeting at his office. But he was the only one there."

"No." Siegel's tone changed again. "I didn't hear anything about this. I would have—"

"They called me directly. His secretary, and told me to go there at ten o'clock."

Siegel was quiet for a moment. In a voice muffled with sadness he finally said, "You should always let me handle your appointments."

"They called my home."

"Well—" More silence. "Wednesday at—"

"But I don't know what to do, Siegel," Anna cried into the phone. I am a stranger here. I don't know anyone. You're all I've got!" Her English failed her.

"All right." His voice became firmer, as if he had made a decision. "I want you to come in. I'll be here most of the day. I know this is serious. It's difficult. But I've dealt with this before. Come see me today. As soon as you can."

He gave her hope. That was what she needed. But the next person she talked to needed to be Ferdie.

Morton

SATURDAY WAS USUALLY a workday for Mort, but he made an effort to keep it short, and if possible just make calls from home. Saturday night he and Elaine would go to a party, or the symphony and a party, or perhaps a premiere and a party. So he liked to start the day by reconnecting with his wife, since he would often have barely seen her since the previous Sunday. It made things smoother. Sunday would be Son-day, with Brian and Gordon. They would go up to Big Bear, or fly model airplanes, or have a catch. Then they would have the only real family dinner of the week.

He grabbed a cup of coffee and took it to his desk in the little wood-paneled den. This side of the house stayed shady in the morning, which suited him. Sometimes when he came here he would be hungover or exhausted or just out of sorts, and the shade was much more relaxing than streaming sun. He took a small pill bottle from the pocket of his dressing gown, opened it and tapped out two bennies. With that slight tailwind he would need only the single cup of coffee—coffee tended to sour his stomach—and he would get by with the light breakfast Elaine would be serving him. That would usually be a poached or boiled egg, a slice of wheat toast with margarine, a half grapefruit and a small glass of skimmed milk. He would eat this uncomplaining because he knew she was right. He was fifteen pounds overweight—alright, twenty—and Elaine was not an ounce too heavy and in much better shape than he was. So he ate what she gave him, and swam twenty laps in the pool almost every day. He had been a good swimmer since childhood, and it was the only form of exercise he really enjoyed.

Elaine came into the room followed by a maid carrying a

tray from which she served the breakfast items, placing them on the small round table near the window. Elaine took one of the two seats and poured herself coffee from a small pitcher. Mort noticed that he had escaped the grapefruit today. In its place was a small bowl of dark red strawberries. On cue, Elaine said, "The grapefruit and oranges are going away, and it's too early for summer fruits. But these strawberries are excellent."

"Thank you, dear." Mort sat in the other chair and plucked a strawberry from the bowl and into his mouth. "Yes, very good!"

Elaine was almost forty, six years younger than Mort. She was slim, attractive, confident, vivacious and neurotic. She had married Mort for his brains and wit, not for his looks, and certainly not for his character. They would have long, interesting, enjoyably deep and wide-ranging conversations— more in the early years, but still not infrequently today, even though they had long since fallen out of love. And a lot of that talk had to do with the movie business. Elaine was no dilettante.

"Talked to Stowbridge lately?" She knew all about his troubles with the headstrong British director.

"Oh, yes indeed. He talks about everything but the movie."

"And you listen?"

"And listen. And then the last thing before he leaves, I tell him what we're going to do. And he nods his head and smiles. Because I speak with my checkbook."

"Good for you." Elaine smiled with slightly vengeful satisfaction.

What they were really talking about was Stowbridge's stubborn arrogance and massive ego. "And I know he'll do anything to stay here. He doesn't want to go back to filming on the moors or whatever they do over there."

"No, that's obvious. He's now completely a creature of

Hollywood."

They both had their community-property interest at heart. Mort knew that Elaine was thinking of divorcing him. She might even be thinking of it right now. One reason she had not done it yet, he knew, was that he was still floundering financially from the exorbitant cost of his films—speaking of stubborn arrogance and massive ego—and the startup of the new studio. So his next movie would probably cost him half his assets if it was a hit because she would divorce him. If it was a flop, they would probably stay married and probably lose everything. Together.

The phone rang and Mort rose to answer it. It was his answering service.

"Sorry, Mr. Blackwell, but we've got a—"

"That's all right, dear. What have we got?"

"Well, there's a reporter from the *Star* who wants a comment."

She paused as if summoning some needed tactfulness. That put Mort on alert. "Comment about what?"

"On the death of Ken Preston."

Mort was not sure he had heard correctly. "Ken Preston?"

"Yes, sir."

"Died?"

"So the man says. He says that Ken is the husband—"

"I know who he is! When did he die? How?"

"I don't know, sir. I just took the message."

Elaine had stopped eating and sat watching him closely. He turned away from her. "Well, I'll have to find out more before I talk to a reporter. But give me his number."

He hung up the phone. "So much for having a weekend. Kenny Preston was killed. He's Pamela Carr's—"

"Good Lord! By who?"

"I mean he died. I don't know how." Pamela's dark, deep eyes flitted across his inner vision and disappeared.

"This is the boy who's been giving her trouble?"

"She was trying to get up the nerve to divorce him. He said if she did, he'd sabotage our publicity campaign." Mort stood there for a moment, almost physically torn about where to go. Back to breakfast? Or . . . what? Go find Pamela? Go bury the boy? Go write a memo, a press release? For a crazy moment he wondered if this was some kind of revenge by Brooks, the shark to whom Mort still owed thousands of dollars. But that was ridiculous. Why kill someone else to warn him? But maybe it was just a hoax. Again, to warn him.

With no definite direction to go, he sat down again and sipped some juice.

Elaine had stopped eating as well. "Could he really have done that? He's an unknown."

"I didn't want to take a chance because her image is something we've worked very hard to . . ." He let that thought die. "I was trying to get him a New York play, get him out of town."

"Well," she said. "It's too bad."

"Yeah. Now the publicity is going to be a bitch anyway. I just really hope she didn't shoot him."

Elaine frowned at him. "You're kidding."

"No, of course she wouldn't. I hope."

"So he was shot?"

"I don't know. No idea."

Elaine took a sip of coffee and resumed her breakfast. "Why was she divorcing him?"

"He was an ass."

"You can't get a divorce for that."

"Well." Mort tried to recall different kinds of grounds for divorce. "Y'know, mental cruelty."

"Not for that either. It's got to be abandonment, prison, physical assault—" Elaine went silent, and when Mort looked up, she was staring out the window, her face full of loss. "Oh, no," she said. "Not her."

"Not who . . . what?" Mort of course knew exactly what she was talking about, and exactly what he could not admit.

She had raised her hands, pressing them into the sides of her face. "I thought you'd go for the Swede."

"What Swede? What d'ya—"

"Marte."

"She's not Swedish, she's Norwegian. And no, I haven't gone for anybody."

Elaine was looking down at her plate now, looking anywhere but at him. "But maybe she went for you."

"Who?"

"Anyone!" She slammed a fist on the table. The dishes and cutlery rattled. A glass of orange juice fell over and splashed on Mort. "Anyone, God damn you! Any one of your starlets, your bonbons!" She pushed herself up and stalked out of the room, leaving Mort alone with a soggy napkin and a plate of uneaten healthy food. Now all that was left for him to do would be to try to calm her down. They'd been through this minefield before. And he would get her through it again. But it would cost him.

Priscilla

PRISCILLA AWOKE FILLED with resolve. The time had come to step out of the shadows and face reality. Accepting the blame for the failure of the marriage would allow her to make a clean breast. That was what she needed to do. Starting here, at the doctor's refuge. Then her chat in the morning with the writer, Lyman, had helped. Not because of anything he said, but just to realize somehow that a person has to move on. It was kind of Scarlett O'Hara moment. Tomorrow is another day.

But she never got the chance. Because now it did not matter.

When Doc Robbie came to her room it was early afternoon. He sat down on the little couch. She sat next to him. He spoke softly, hesitantly. Not at all like his usual approach. "I'm sorry I didn't tell you sooner. I didn't know it was going to proceed like this."

Priscilla had no idea what he was talking about and she began to be frightened.

"The coroner took the body, and I was waiting to get some more information."

"It's Ken."

"Yes. You knew?"

He continued to talk. Priscilla no longer heard.

✧　✧　✧

THE NIGHT SHE signed the contract with Blackwell Productions, Ken took her to celebrate with dinner at the Stork Club, by the end of which there was no denying that he was very uneasy about the changes they were facing. Of course they had dreamed of success, but always as a couple, as a team, and at first she thought his male ego was perhaps injured by her suddenly being the big earner, even though she had not done a thing yet.

"No," he said. "It's just the fact that our future is now sort of out of control. Out of *our* control. We'll be heading to California before long. Or you will be. I have to finish the season here. Even though we don't need the money any more, it's good for my reputation to do so. And it's my best chance of getting something better. Probably not a personal services contract with Morton Blackwell."

A little sarcasm had crept in there at the end. "Well, I think he might sign you too. I made it clear that I'm married, and we want to work together. He told me he'd find me something here."

"Like what?"

"Well, I don't know." Priscilla felt a little flustered. "I just signed the contract today."

"He's going to want you in films." Ken nodded with unearned wisdom. "I know it, and once you get out there, you'll forget about me."

"How can you say that?" Priscilla snapped. "Who do you think you're talking to?" Realizing that was the wrong approach, she reached across to him with both arms, and touched his cheek. "Never, darling. Never."

But in fact, it had already begun. Morton Blackwell was a commanding presence, full of charm, generosity, humor and energy. He could be tremendously focused, and that could overwhelm the person he focused on. That could be intimidating, or even somewhat threatening. At her next meeting with Blackwell, a few days later, Priscilla sat riveted as he recounted his father's catastrophic business failure, which had scarred Mort badly just as he approached the age when he should have been setting out in pursuit of his own dreams. After that he no longer thought of dreams, but of conquests. And he had succeeded, whatever it took, every step of the way, until he reached the pinnacle.

Mort quickly decided to bring Priscilla to Hollywood. Like Ken said. And as Ken no doubt feared, Mort installed her in a very nice room in an excellent hotel, and then got her into bed in that very nice room. But what Ken probably did not suspect was that it was Priscilla who seduced Morton. She thought it would be a one time thing, and that it would open a door for her. She already had a contract, but many people had contracts. She wanted make sure the head of the studio did not forget her. This was wisdom she had gained in dressing room tales by actresses, of the peaks and valleys, the ladders and tunnels and detours of a theatrical career for a woman. Sometimes you have to lay it on the line. Priscilla had only done it once before, with a very successful New York agent. It was a short, unappetizing encounter. And she did get a job out of it—not the part she wanted, but still a role in a Broadway show. She played it in Providence and Philly, where the show died. But still it was a Broadway show with Broadway talent and production. It got her going. And she never saw or talked to that agent again.

That was not to be with Mort, who went hook, line, sinker, pole, reel, boat for her. Priscilla was not prepared for that. Within days he had her meeting people, being coached, manicured, groomed, doing screen tests, makeup tests, wardrobe tests. And at nights he would call frequently and come by late. Sometimes these visits would end with sex. More often, he just wanted to talk and be with her.

✧　✧　✧

"SO YOU WERE here Friday night. The doctor said you checked in about six p.m."

"You don't really sign in," Priscilla told him. "I have been a patient, I guess you call it, of the doctor for, oh, a month or so. This, though, was an emergency sort of situation. Ken had come to my hotel. He had been drinking, and he was very . . . demanding. I had to get away from him. I arranged to spend the night here."

The detective had a large, nobly cut head. In ancient Rome he would have been a centurion. And he had these very fashionable-looking horn-rim glasses. He was sitting in the room with her. Priscilla had not left since Doc brought the news about Kenny. She had been waiting for someone to tell her what to do, but at the same time she feared what that might be.

She realized the detective was saying something. "I'm sorry, what?"

"You were staying at a hotel. So you have not been living together? For a while?"

She felt emotion balling up high in her chest. She nodded. "I'm divorcing him."

"I see. And did he know this Friday—last night? You had told him?"

"I think he got the papers Thursday or Friday, but I'm not sure. He did not mention that."

The detective scratched the corner of his jaw. "That's tough. Was he an emotional person? He would take that news pretty hard, wouldn't he?"

"Oh yes."

"You two hadn't really talked about it."

"Oh no. It would have been impossible."

"Because he's, what? Too domineering? Too sensitive? Too . . .?"

"Because he would have talked me out of it. Surely. I know it. I just couldn't confront him, or I'd just fall apart."

"I see."

The detective looked down at his notebook for a few moments. Someone was talking out on the patio. Priscilla couldn't tell who was talking or what they were saying. But surely it had to be about her. How could it not be?

"So," said the centurion. "This is a proud guy, very

committed to you and the marriage, and out of nowhere—would that be fair to say?—out of nowhere he gets this kick in the teeth. So he starts drinking, and he drinks too much, maybe way too much. And he decides, what the hell, I can't do this anymore, and takes some sleeping pills."

"No. Definitely not. He was raised religious. And he actually told me once that suicide was a sin. I think he said it was the greatest sin."

"So do you think he took some accidentally, or maybe he was making a cry for help, or trying to make you feel guilty. After all, he called a friend of his who came over, but it was too late."

This description was devastating, with its necessary imagining of Ken's last hours. Priscilla shook her head. "No. That kind . . . of thing would be totally unlike him."

"Well." The detective had been leaning closer to her. Now he sat back in his chair, raised his arms and turned his palms up. "We know he died of the alcohol and pills. There is one other possibility, and only one. Someone drugged him. We know there was a sedative in his system. We found a bottle of sleeping pills in the house. Was he using these regularly?"

"I don't know. We've been separated for several months. He's never taken sleeping pills regularly since we've been married, that I know of."

"But he did have some?"

"If you say so, but I don't know."

"All right," said the detective. He smiled. The interview was over. "Please believe me, I regret your loss. I'm sorry to have to bother you at this time."

"That's alright."

He stood up and moved toward the door. "I hate to see young guys die. I saw enough of that in the war."

"Thank you," she said.

He extended his hand and Priscilla took it. "Thank you. We won't be bothering you anymore."

He turned and walked out, closing the door behind him.

CHAPTER SEVEN
Sunday, April 20

Lyman

LYMAN DID NOT see her that night, though he heard soft, occasional noises coming from her room. He did not see her the next morning but did see Dr. Rosenstone, in his office off the dining room.

"We're having a group session this morning. I think you should be there. I think you'll really get along."

"Little dogie. Sure. Anything. Sessions on Sunday?"

The doctor was looking through a file that lay on the desk in front of him. Lyman assumed it was his file. It was not thick. "It's the only day a lot of people can come. Those who work in the studios."

But Lyman had something on his mind, and, as usual, he didn't hesitate to blurt it out. "This Priscilla, or Pamela. She's an actress?"

The doctor's expression passed into professional bemusement. "Yes, very much so."

"She's good? She's big?"

"A neophyte. She's on her first picture, but I gather it's a big role."

"Well, as nice a young woman as you'd ever want to meet. I talked to her yesterday morning. She's having troubles with her husband. Also an actor?"

"A very nice young lady. Without question. But you know I can't discuss patients with anyone, even in a court of law."

Lyman considered that statement. It was much firmer than it needed to be. He had only been speaking in the most general terms about someone he'd met, not prying into her file. And what was that guff about a court of law?

He went back to his cottage. It had been a bit more than three weeks since he had worked. In that time he had not tasted anything liquid but water, coffee, juice, and soda pop. Maybe tomorrow he should call Fred Sheldrake and get back into the swing of things.

In fact, he needed to go to work. Without Tina in his life, without Demon Rum in his life, the hollow would have to be filled with work.

At eleven he walked out to find the group session. Some people seemed to be gathering under the veranda, near the jungle garden. Lyman went to investigate. A thrillingly handsome young man leaned against a stucco pillar, hands in pockets, at ease. Lyman would learn his problem was twofold: that he was homosexual, and that he was not ashamed of it, or particularly interested in hiding it. These characteristics were considered either commendable self-assurance or self-destructive impulses, depending on the situation. Sitting on a rattan chair was a woman who Lyman knew as an actress but who was now directing, who worried about how to assert the necessary authority without losing her femininity. And there was an alcoholic writer (fortyish, balding) and a second alcoholic writer (thirtyish, with her dark hair pulled back in a short, severe ponytail).

And then there was Zerxes. Lyman got no clue as to what he exactly did, but he was obviously as connected to the industry as the rest of them. Zerxes was a force of nature, a smooth and nimble torrent of language and expressions that was both sly and extremely informative. He seemed to know everything about everyone.

Lyman's initial impression was: flaming faggot. But after

five minutes of conversation with Zerxes (which would always be at least 4:35 of listening) it became clear that he was very heterosexual. So Lyman decided that he could be just flaming, without the other part.

The group was not unhelpful. At first it seemed like an old-fashioned vaudeville routine, where nobody listens to anybody else. Lyman related somewhat to the lady director trying to succeed as both an artist and a human being, a challenge Lyman felt some directors had given up on, based on his personal knowledge of a few of them. And he was impressed with the handsome young man's honesty. The two writer-alkies he found about equally tiresome. Zerxes alone— besides the doctor—seemed to really be listening and responding to the others throughout the session, giving only oblique tidbits about himself.

After Doc left, the group lounged around, except for the directress, who left immediately, heels tocking on the flagstones of the patio.

Zerxes leaned toward Lyman and muttered, "She's in there, you know."

Lyman followed his gaze to the cottages on the other side of the pool. "You mean Pris—"

"Of course, the poor woman."

"What do you mean?"

"You know, the husb—" Zerxes leaned closer and spoke even lower. "He killed himself or something."

"It was in the *Star* this a.m." The male writer, Casper, was eavesdropping. "They managed to get him into the lede, but just barely. Kenny Something, an aspiring actor and husband of Pamela Carr, star of the new Blackwell Studios picture, blew his brains out, or what have you. The poor schmuck."

Lyman recoiled in shock. "Good lord!"

Zerxes asked the writer, "Have the cops been here?"

"I dunno. Ask him. He's staying here." Casper flicked a

couple of fingers toward Lyman.

"I have no idea." Lyman recalled his talk with the doctor not two hours ago. "When was this, that he killed himself?"

"Yesterday. No maybe it would have to have been Friday, late at night." Casper shrugged.

Everybody in the circle was now listening.

"Yeah," said Zerxes. "Yeah, it's a Morton Blackwell picture, and you know what they say about him."

Lyman did not know. Here he was sitting with these seeming Hollywood insiders, and he didn't feel like a Hollywood insider at all. Yet he was, wasn't he? "No, what do they say?"

"That he's filming her during the day and he's—" Zerxes did a bird call—"her at night. And the husband either eats that or profits from it. And not just her. I guess this time the husband couldn't do either one."

Lyman tried to separate this very sad story from the bizarre telling. Had this already happened the morning he met her? Yesterday? No, the woman he talked to had been full of sadness and hope, not terrible tragedy. Lyman looked over there. He could feel her in the little cottage. He could feel her agony.

Priscilla

PRISCILLA'S RESTLESS THOUGHTS raced from emotion to emotion, back and forth through time, from place to place and face to face. Her loved ones. Her mother. Ken. She thought of the first night they spent together, swinging wildly from bashfulness to overwhelming need. He was a wiry, muscular man. He would be perfect in an Army movie, digging a foxhole, in an undershirt, sweating, his dog tags hanging out. That first night she did not care about his kindness or his gentle soul, just his body, his face. He had ears that stuck out a little at the top, and a crooked grin, and an awkward intensity.

It was torture to think of him alive and happy. There had been plenty of unhappiness, certainly, but the image that would not leave her alone was that marvelous smile of his, that laugh that sounded almost phony when he really cut loose.

She should never have slept with Morton Blackwell. That one act had started an avalanche, had unleashed the older man's energy and trained it on her. Her dream of getting to the top, the ambition that she had shared with Ken, had been taken over by Morton Blackwell and become even stronger. And Ken, who also loved her completely, was left behind with no career, no glory, no woman, no wife.

With Ken, all had been physical, vocal. Gesture. Smile. Frown. After all, they were both actors, performers, and love between them was a performance, though a heartfelt one. With Mort, it was all mental, ethereal. Greatness, glory, legend, and she was, in a way, a prize to him as much as a person. Just showing the world: he had done it all, succeeded in business, made the greatest movies, and captured the most beautiful woman. That had not bothered her. In fact she had let herself be fooled and seduced by his vision and charisma, all the time knowing how false it was. Tinseltown. And she had let herself think it was all real.

Priscilla looked out at the waves breaking on the deserted beach. Darkness had come, the traffic on the highway behind her was gone. Now she would become a legend indeed, but a very small one. She would join Aïda, Cleopatra, Madame Bovary and Hedda Gabler—women who sacrificed themselves on the altar of their guilt.

She knew Romeo and Juliet by heart, having seen it multiple times since childhood, including in the wings of her parents' theater. Once, as she stood there offstage watching with her father, at the climax of the play, just before he stood up to lower the curtain, he said, "You know, it was guilt done her in."

Poor Juliet—it was true. But the tragic character Priscilla most related to was Hedda Gabler. She had seen Katharine Cornell do the role in Chicago some years ago, Hedda paying for her sins—each and every vivid one—with her life. That had been the image bouncing around in her unconscious when she was told of Ken's death: Løvbeog, sent to his death by the actions of a cold, ambitious woman.

Her heart soared with pure love for the innocent and hopeful young man who had been so determined to win her, who thought he had won her. She had not deserved him, and she knew that the kind of dreamy, fiery passion they had shared was gone from her life. But she also knew that she was like Juliet, that in death Ken had sealed their love forever and willed her a gravestone she would have to drag through the rest of her days.

There was only one way to be free of that, but it involved another betrayal. She could no longer hurt Ken, except by being the one who knew him best, who carried his memory closest, and taking that knowledge to her own grave so soon after his death. This was doubly cruel since she had not been with him when he needed her most, had in fact been plotting how to get rid of him. He had given her freedom as a gift, and now she was throwing that away.

Now it was time. She opened the door and pulled herself out of the car. She did not feel the ground, was not aware of her steps. There was a short but steep bank, and she seemed to float down to the sand and toward the water. It would be cold, and she was glad of that. Her self-loathing was bottomless.

But now it seemed she was no longer walking, but lying there on the sand, which should have been cold but was somehow warm, and she was looking over her shoulder at the stars. She wanted to get up and continue to the water, and then it seemed that she was, sliding over the beach like the flat, shimmering end of a wave, returning to the sea.

Then she was on her back, the stars spinning overhead, and everything began to slip away.

Act One Curtain

CHAPTER EIGHT
Monday, April 21

Lyman

THE NEXT MORNING, Monday, Lyman was up earlier than usual, his mind absorbed with the idea of going back to work. He still missed Tina, felt the hollow place in his soul that would never go away. But he felt sober, strong, ready to re-enter life. He would leave Doc Rosenstone's compound, or playground, or whatever it was. He would call Fred Sheldrake. He would get back in the game.

While dressing, Lyman heard a knock on the door. He slipped on a shirt and opened the door to no one. He leaned to look out, and was surprised to see, just a few feet away, Dr. Rosenstone knocking again on Priscilla's door.

The doctor glanced over at Lyman. "Good morning." After a second he added, "Have you seen her?"

"No." Lyman stepped outside. "Not since . . . but I know she's there. I can hear her."

The doctor nodded and softly rapped again. Lyman expected the door to open and was surprised when it did not.

"She was here last night?"

"Yeah. I guess." Now Lyman was doubting. "I heard someone in there."

"Okay."

They stood waiting for another a full minute. The noise of the surrounding city filtered into the doctor's leafy refuge. The sound had a Monday feel to it, and it reminded Lyman of his day's mission. He was about to go back inside and finish dressing when the doctor pulled out a key and unlocked the door. He pushed it open six inches. "Miss Carr? Mrs. Preston?"

Nothing but cool silence came through the opening, and the doctor pushed on the door and stepped in. Lyman felt compelled to follow. The doctor stood in the middle of a room nearly identical to Lyman's but showing even less evidence of habitation. Through an open door, Lyman could see a neatly made bed. He said. "She wasn't here. I guess I was wrong."

The doctor shook his head and Lyman realized that the man was glad he had not walked in on a dead patient. He pushed open the bathroom door and looked in. Apparently there was nobody lying in the tub with slit wrists. Lyman immediately felt ashamed of himself for thinking of a real person, a very warm and sympathetic person, as the corpse in a hardboiled drama.

"Okay," said the doctor. "But you think she was here earlier in the day yesterday, maybe in the afternoon?"

"Yes, I'm sure of that. I heard her voice."

"Talking to someone else?"

"I don't know. I can't say that. I only know I heard her voice, I wasn't paying attention, I turned on the bath and didn't hear anything after that."

"Alright. Er, people are free to come and go. And they don't have to report. Though we do prefer it. And by the way, that's true for you, too."

"I was going to talk to you about that. I don't know exactly what arrangements have been made and I'd like to continue our meetings, but I think it's time for me to get back on my feet, start earning my keep."

"Alright. Come by my office, say, later this morning. Just let me first see if I can find my lost lamb."

"Certainly." Lyman could see that his exit was going to

happen. Soon. He had breakfast and used the telephone in the reception hall to call Sheldrake.

"That is great news," said the producer. "I've heard good things about you and how it's going."

Now Lyman knew at least one of the arrangements. He could not work up much umbrage about being reported on to the man who was footing the bills.

"Tell you what," said Sheldrake. "Let's have lunch. Tomorrow. Welcome home, right?"

Now that that was settled, Lyman ambled over to Doc's office, his head pleasantly occupied with thoughts of the future and the specifics of ending his odyssey, finding a new place to live, wondering if his car, which had been in the garage for a month—he hoped!—would start up.

Rosenstone was in his office, the door open, talking on the phone. Lyman waited discreetly, not listening—*even in a court of law*—, he remembered. When the call ended, Lyman leaned into the doorway. "Did you ever find her?"

Rosenstone looked up. "No. The gardener said she took all her stuff and went home last night. So." He shrugged. "So thank you for letting me know you're going."

"No problem," said Lyman.

Anna

SIEGEL'S OFFICE WAS a small, one-story stucco cottage with a Mexican veranda facing a quiet, narrow street off Sunset Boulevard. The street was lined with tall trees that rustled when the breeze blew, as it was blowing now. Next to this quaint bungalow stood a steel warehouse, and on the other side of the warehouse could be heard the constant noise and activity from Sunset Blvd.

Anna took note of all this as she walked with Siegel under the trees, up the street. He had surprised her by coming out of the office and offering his arm, guiding her across the veranda, down the steps and into a leisurely stroll toward the quiet end of the street, just making small talk at first. He asked about Ferdie, about Anna's parents, who were still living in Frankfurt in West Germany, as it was now beginning to be called. They hoped to come to the U.S., dreamed of seeing their daughter in a Hollywood movie.

She let go of his arm and they continued slowly up the street. Siegel had other European clients, he knew how to do business in the seemingly relaxed and deliberate way they preferred. The noise from Sunset became swallowed up by the rustling of the trees and the chatter of birds.

"I don't want to know what happened," he finally said. "All I want to know is, are you all right?"

"Yes." Anna shrugged. "Sure."

"He didn't physically harm you, or, you know . . ."

"No." Anna didn't want to talk about it and hardly knew how to.

"I'm sorry. He's a pig. Who else have you told? Your husband?"

"No. I'm afraid of what he might do."

They had come to a home that had been converted, like Siegel's, into a cozy small office. Her he stopped walking. There were some houses on the street that people obviously still lived in, including one where she could hear a baby crying for a few minutes. Others had been converted into offices, and the one they stood in front of now was a particularly beautiful example. Behind a low rock wall, a verdant flower and fern garden filled the space in front of the house. A huge, dark tree, an oak of some kind, perhaps, spread great limbs over the garden, most of the house and almost half the street.

Siegel sat on the stone wall. He combed back his thick, tightly curly gray hair with his fingers. "Okay, first of all, let me say that I'm so sorry this happened to you. I try to take care of my people." He made a chopping motion with one hand. "But it's impossible with this kind of *schvantz*."

"I know that." She sat down next to him.

"If I had known about this meeting, believe me, I would never have let you go alone. Always let me know. It's my job to protect you."

"I know. I did not suspect anything. I thought there would be someone else there. And then he was on the phone for … for hours, it seemed like. I almost fell asleep."

"I've heard things about him." He tipped his head left and right. "But you hear things about everybody."

The anger came rushing up from deep inside her. "But what do I do!"

"Okay." Siegel gave her a long, serious stare. He looked up into the branches of the tree. Then he began speaking softly and slowly. "Okay. You want revenge. You want justice. You're angry, and I don't blame you." He pointed over his shoulder with his thumb at the house behind them. "This is a lawyer's office. We can go in there right now. He's a good friend of mine. He's very good. He will help you. I will help you. We'll take it to the police."

Anna realized this was not just a pleasant stroll under the trees. Siegel had brought her here to make a decision. "Is that what I should do?"

"It won't be easy." He leanded close to her. "What will probably happen is, that they will question Blackwell and he will deny it. So then you need some other kind of proof. Is there any evidence other than your word?"

She felt a flash of anger that she should be doubted. That the truth was not enough. "The security guards saw me come in and saw me leave."

"Did you say anything to them?"

"Not as I was leaving. But they know I was there, at least." As she walked out she had a dress with buttons ripped off. But she had been trying to hide that from anyone who might look, including the guards. These little bits of evidence seemed to prove, if they proved anything at all, that she was lucky to have gotten away without being choked and raped. Getting sick might have been the only thing that saved her from that.

They sat together on the wall in silence for a moment, Anna filled with disgust in the realization that she would just have to take this. She had come to Hollywood filled with hope, but just as much to escape the weight of brutal history and suffocating hypocrisy in Danzig, in Berlin, even in Paris. The Hakenkreuz, the hammer and sickle. Now the sunshine, the open sky, the distant mountains seemed to mock her delusions. There is no escape in life, there is no joy and no justice. We are nothing but flies on a window screen yearning to get out if we are inside, or get in if we are outside.

"Here is what I know," said Siegel. "This place, this town, is as dark and devious as a Renaissance kingdom, where the rich and powerful defend themselves and attack each other with lies and murder. You are under contract to this man, which is almost a blood oath. He can bury you so deep you will never see the light of day."

"I know. I know."

"Morton Blackwell—people who don't know, think he's one of those rich and powerful ones. But I know he's not. This so-called studio of his is hocked up to the shingles. His marriage is shaky and he's made a lot of enemies." Siegel jerked his thumb behind him again. "Now we can go in right now and get the process started, and maybe it will work. Or, you can keep your dagger clean and sharp and out of sight. And wait. Wait. Wait until he's weak and desperate, and then gut him." Siegel made a knife of his finger and drew it up the front of his shirt. "That's the Hollywood way."

Anna studied the earnest face of her agent. All her life men she barely knew had been giving her advice she did not want, and here was another one. You can go ten thousand miles, buy a brand-new automobile and have dinner with the President of the United States and the Pope, and nothing is different. "So that's all I can do? Just wait, and hope?"

Siegel shrugged. "Sometimes the gods intervene. That guy has a new problem. He made a big splash about finding this innocent young girl to play a saint in his new movie. And the innocent young girl's husband just killed himself. If it gets in the gossip columns, he'll get roasted."

"Who killed himself?"

"Kenny something. The husband of Pamela Carr. No one's ever heard of her. But they'll hear of her now." He shrugged. "Maybe."

Anna glimpsed a flash of light. "When was this?"

Siegel thought for a moment. "Friday, I believe. Or Saturday. I read it in the *Reporter* Saturday night."

The round stones of the wall beneath her were hard and uneven, causing her to teeter uncertainly rather than firmly sit. For that reason, and for other reasons, she stood up, took Siegel's hand and pulled him up.

"I will think about this," she said. "Let's go back."

Dr. Rosenstone

Barbiturates are organic compounds used in medicine as sedatives or sleeping pills. The first important drug in the family was phenobarbital, developed in 1912. Barbiturates act by depressing the central nervous system particularly in certain portions of the brain, though they tend to depress the functioning of all the body's tissues. The prolonged use of barbiturates—especially secobarbital and pentobarbital—may cause the development of a tolerance to them and require amounts much larger than the original therapeutic dose. Denial of a barbiturate to the habitual user may precipitate a withdrawal syndrome that is indicative of physiological dependence on the drug. An overdose of barbiturates can result in coma and even death due to severe depression of the central nervous and respiratory systems.

Barbiturates became known as "goofballs" about the time of the Second World War, when they were used to help soldiers cope with combat conditions. Soon the abuse of barbiturate drugs became highly prevalent in Western societies, and they were often taken in combination with other substances. Alcohol greatly intensifies the depressant effect of barbiturates, and barbiturates taken with alcohol became a common agent in suicide cases.

Tranquilizers are a class of drugs that are used to reduce anxiety, fear, tension, agitation, and related states of mental disturbance. Tranquilizers are of two types. Major tranquilizers, which are also known as antipsychotic agents, or neuroleptics, are used to treat major states of mental disturbance in schizophrenics and other psychotic patients. By contrast, minor tranquilizers, which are also known as anti-anxiety agents, are used to treat milder states of anxiety and tension in healthy individuals or people with less serious mental disorders.

These drugs have a calming effect and eliminate both the physical and psychological effects of anxiety or fear. Besides the treatment of anxiety disorders, they are widely used to relieve the strain and worry arising from stressful circumstances in daily life. The first tranquilizer, benzodiazepine, was an immediate success when first introduced in the 1940s, and revolutionized perceptions of anxiety and its treatment. Benzodiazepines resemble barbiturates in their side effects: sleepiness, drowsiness, reduced alertness, and unsteadiness of gait. Though less dangerous than barbiturates, they can produce physical dependency even in moderate dosages, and the body develops a tolerance to them, necessitating the use of progressively larger doses. The effects of mixing with alcohol are only slightly less dangerous than with barbiturates.

Doc Rosenstone put down the book. Fred Allen was telling jokes on the radio, but the doctor wasn't laughing. Alone in his tower he mulled over an evil scheme.

The mansion had two entrances. The rooms on the ground floor were devoted to his professional life. The private entrance and upper floor were where he lived. Alone, except for visits by his girlfriend, and the children from his defunct marriage. This rather spacious apartment was his castle keep, where his mind roamed free, and he could hatch his evil schemes. Like the one aimed at his colleague and rival Eloise Kness. It was underhanded, scurrilous, devious, and might be great for his own career. It was also dangerous, on the level of professional gossip and Psychoanalytic Institute politics, and it might backfire, but Rosenstone couldn't resist.

Eloise had come to L.A. from the East just before the war and had taken the local psychiatric world by storm. She was a brilliant, lively, sympathetic woman who, in Rosenstone's opinion, gathered patients by feeding their egos, encouraging their grievances, and helping their careers through her network of contacts, which included studio heads, producers, agents and money men and their wives, siblings, children, and lovers.

And it wasn't just jealousy of her client list that fueled Rosenstone's disdain. He and a number of his associates considered her hand-holding, fresh-baked-cookie approach to be therapeutically useless, if not actually unethical. From Freud on down, one of the first tenets of psychoanalysis was to maintain a professional detachment from the patient, to be a sounding board, a guide, but never a buddy, never a collaborator or co-conspirator, never a mother and only the sternest type of father.

And never a friend. Eloise went to dinner with her patients and their families. She went to parties, fund-raisers, tennis tournaments and movie premieres. Rosenstone could just about see her doing sleepovers with her patients' families, sleeping in the daughter's room, padding around in carpet slippers and a fuzzy robe, dropping analytical insights as she trundled in for breakfast.

And then there was the narcotics issue. Rosenstone knew for an almost fact that she was a willing dispenser of sleeping pills, painkillers, stimulants, and tranquilizers. This pharmaceutical approach indicated the bankruptcy of her therapeutic ideas. Drugs were a way to smooth things over, make everything alright. But they all had the potential for dependence or addiction, and once that set in, their only purpose was to stave off the anxiety of withdrawal.

Elaine could prescribe these drugs because she was an M.D. Rosenstone was not, of course. He followed Freud in his belief that psychoanalysis was a full-fledged discipline of its own, not a branch of medicine like podiatry or urology.

For these reasons, he thought Eloise Kness should be brought down a peg. He didn't want to destroy her—he doubted that he even could. But down a peg, that would give him some satisfaction, and almost certainly, some new patients.

And he had an ally.

"Joe, I'm calling to see how you're doing."

"I'm alright, Doc. A lot better than Kenny."

There was the writer again, always with the punchline handy. "Good. I know it had to be tough on you. It would be tough on anyone, walking in on your friend—"

"Yeah, it was. We're a lot alike, but there was something just, inside him, something that that couldn't quite click, it seemed. He shoulda been seeing a psychiatrist."

"As a matter of fact, he was. Didn't he tell you?"

"No, we never talked about that. When we got together it was, y'know, for fun. To get away from our problems. Who was he seeing?"

"Well," said Rosenstone. "Perhaps telling you would violate confidentiality, since you're a reporter."

"Off the record. I'm also his friend, and a former patient of yours. And by the way I'm grateful to you. You really helped me."

"Why, thank you for saying so, Joe. Some of my most gratifying outcomes have been with you war veterans. I can't give you a name, but I can tell you something that is bothering me. And of course this is strictly off the record. I'm telling you only as a friend of Ken's."

"Sure, I get it."

Rosenstone hesitated. "Have the police or the coroner said the cause of death?"

"No, they're waiting on blood tests. Believe me, I'm calling them every day."

This statement helped reassure Rosenstone that Joe could be an ally. "Well, I believe that Ken was addicted to barbiturates. Sleeping pills. When a person becomes addicted to these, it has nothing to do with sleep. They use them to calm down, to relax, and eventually to fight off the physical effects of withdrawal. Taking these pills becomes almost like having a stiff drink, except you have to keep doing it every day. And when these pills are mixed with alcohol, they become quite dangerous."

"Yeah, the detective told me that it looked like a drug case. Which was shocking to me. I never saw him out of control. I mean he'd go on a toot once in awhile, but nothing like drugs. He was too clean-cut for that.

"Oh, they're insidious."

"Who are?" said Joe. "The pills or the people? Jesus. What a fucked up . . . How was he getting them? From the shrink, I assume, or his kindly old family doctor."

Now that Joe had been given the scent, if he was truly a reportorial bloodhound, should have little trouble finding out who Kenny Preston's shrink was. "That's why I'm sure you'll understand I really can't mention any names. I have always refused to suggest drugs for my patients, because giving them to patients who are Q.E.D. unstable or unhappy is the equivalent of putting a gun in their hands."

"No, I never knew, or even suspected. How is Priscilla?"

"Well," Rosenstone felt a little tickle of uncertainty. She still hadn't returned from wherever she'd gone. "She's bereft, and blames herself, of course."

"She sure should," Joe said with an emotion that caught Rosenstone by surprise. "I know she's your patient, Doc, but what a bitch. What a self-centered, selfish bitch. If Ken killed himself, he did it for her"

"I understand your feelings. All I can say is that she cares deeply for him and is taking this very hard."

"And that asshole—"

"No." Rosenstone stopped him. "I can't talk about any of that."

"But I can. That asshole. It's the oldest story in Hollywood. The big shot takes advantage of a starstruck girl, and the hell with everything else. Not that the girls are innocent. Their pussies clamp down on anything that has a contract attached to it."

Joe paused for breath. Rosenstone let him.

"Sorry," he went on. "But I've seen this one or twelve too many times. But it all starts with the Mort Blackwells and the other heartless bastards who have the power."

Rosenstone let the rant lay there. He was now in a therapy session. "Yes, it's an unequal system. It's unfair. And people get hurt."

"What I hate is that I can't do anything about it. We have to live in the real world. We're vassals of these people—you as much as I. We're the hangers-on, the retinue. Because we're all addicted to the myth of creation, of renewal, of rebirth into a higher . . . something something something."

Doc Rosenstone heard again the writer coming out, but he also heard both the sadness and the truth of what the writer said.

Morton

MORTON BLACKWELL PUSHED a button and the sliding glass doors between the living room and the balcony rolled open. The room where Morton stood was quickly bathed in cool fresh air. He scooped ice into a cut-glass highball tumbler and poured in expensive scotch from the matching cut-glass decanter. At least he assumed it was expensive scotch—he couldn't definitely know since he did not fill the decanter, but it damn well better be the stuff he had paid for. He took a swallow and stared out at the darkening evening. And why is cut-glass so expensive? He'd wondered about that. And what made one glass "crystal," and another glass just, glass?

He took another swallow of the scotch and tried to calm down. Pamela had been AWOL from the studio that morning, and he'd had people looking for her all day. They checked hospitals, jails, police departments and known acquaintances under new name, married name, maiden name. Nothing had turned up.

And he had another problem. His attorney had called in the afternoon. The police wanted to interview him in connection with the death of Kenny Preston.

"What about it?" Mort asked. "What am I supposed to know?"

"They didn't give me any other information," said the lawyer, whose name was Hester. "They're going to let me know when they want to see you, and we'll go topgether. I'm sure it's a routine cleaning up. Probably related to Miss Carr, who was his wife."

Mort walked out onto the balcony. The dark shadows of the canyon below gave way to the lights of the city spread out in the distance. People kept telling him that Pamela was

Ken's wife. He already knew that. And so did the police. He had to wonder what was really going on here. Who knew he was having an affair with her? Had *secreted her away* in a *love nest*, was how the tabloids would put it. Who knew Pamela had called him just about the time her husband was dying? Should he admit that call if they asked him? Should he admit to the affair? The story in the *Star* said police suspected a drug overdose but that there had been no determination if it was accidental, or suicide, or some other cause. What could that mean? Of course in the *Star* every story hinted at the possibility of scandal, of foul play, of a conspiracy by the rich and powerful etc. etc.

But the question remained: why would a young man like Ken Preston do such a thing, either accidentally or on purpose? That's what the police and the press would want to know.

Why? Because Preston was losing her. Why now? Because she had just filed for divorce. Why was he losing her? Because she was in love with Mort. He had won her heart, and Kenny had lost it. Mort could not help that. He had won, Kenny had lost. For just a moment Mort allowed himself a jab of anger. The man had killed himself because he was a sore loser. It was an act of vindictiveness and envy.

No, of course it wasn't. It was a tragedy of a very classic, human kind. Like all true tragedy it was self-inflicted. Kenny could have picked himself up, dusted himself off, and got on with his life. He chose not to do that.

Of course, the other part of the triangle was Pamela, and where the hell was Pamela? Why had she disappeared? For the moment Mort decided to believe that she had gone, grief-stricken, home to her mama. She had told him once she was from . . . well, somewhere in the Midwest. And one place he had not checked was the train station. And also the airport. He would get someone on that.

In the meantime, if asked by Elaine, or the police, he

could deny the affair completely, or at least deny he had talked to her that night. But would that be wise? Was there a way that they could trace his calls from work? He had made a dozen calls that night, like every night. But then, he now remembered, the phone had gone on the fritz. And then he had gone home. He'd driven himself. What time was that? He wasn't sure. He didn't actually remember the drive or getting home. It would make his life simpler now if Lin had driven him and could therefore vouch for his location and the time. But he had dismissed Lin for the evening, hoping to go over to see Pamela.

There was a hum behind him, and a rolling sound which meant the glass doors were closing. He turned and saw Elaine had just come in and was snapping on a table lamp, oblivious to his presence. He stepped into the room ahead of the closing doors.

She looked up. "Oh! You're home."

"Yes."

"Early."

"It's this thing with Pamela. She's disappeared. I've had people beating the bushes all day." He shrugged, suddenly feeling old and fat and tired. "And the police want to talk to me."

Her face went hard. "Why on earth? What could you possibly tell them?"

"I don't know. I'm afraid now that she may have had something to do with his death. She disappeared the same night he died."

"Maybe she's dead, too."

Mort felt a bolt of rage which he knew he absolutely had to suppress. "No, I don't think it's that."

"Why not?"

Mort tipped his glass up and got only a few drops of water from the melting ice. He would try a gambit. "I spoke to her Friday night."

"Really."

"Yeah. Just checking in, since she's been on loan-out I wanted to catch up on what she's doing. We're considering projects for her, and I wanted to touch base."

Elaine was holding some letters she'd brought in from the mailbox. She pretended to read the envelopes. "That sounds very businesslike, except for it being in the middle of the night."

"Come on. You know how late I work."

"But not what you do. Are your starlets usually awake when you call?"

Mort went to the bar and put ice and a small swig of scotch in a glass. He handed it to her and then refilled his own glass. She sipped hers.

"There's no reason for you to get all huffy," said Mort. "I am not doing anything that should embarrass you or make you jealous. I'm just a working stiff with long hours at the shop."

Elaine turned without comment and walked over to the table by the couch, the one with the framed pictures of her and their two sons. She stared at these for a moment.

Mort felt a flash of panic that she was going to turn around and announce the death of their marriage. "Look, I know—"

"Alright," she said. "I'm sorry."

That was it. They would go on. He could go on. "Do you know what time I got home that night? Friday?"

"No. How would I?"

She had been asleep in her own bedroom that night, as she was almost every work night when he got home. He always made a point of not disturbing her.

"Well, do you remember what time you went to bed?"

She thought for a moment, sipping her scotch. "The boys were down at ten thirty and I was right behind them."

"Well, I think I got home at eleven, maybe eleven-fifteen.

I remember thinking you might be up, because I wanted to talk to you about something, about our vacation plans for this summer."

"Really? What about them?"

Mort waved that lie away impatiently. "It doesn't matter. But you didn't hear me or anything?"

She shook her head.

"I must've come right after you fell asleep."

"Morton, I never hear you, you know that. That's why we have separate rooms, so I never hear you."

"Alright. Never mind."

Mort let it go. He had planted the seed. That was all he had to do right now.

CHAPTER NINE
Tuesday-Wednesday

Lyman

HE WAS AT an evening group session when the news came. The doctor held evening groups twice a week, and this one had a different cast than the Sunday group, except for Zerxes. They had almost finished the hour when Rosenstone was interrupted by his assistant to take an important phone call. His expression when he looked at the assistant said i*t had better be important.* And when Rosenstone returned a few minutes later, Lyman was sure it had been, and he thought he knew the subject.

The doctor tried to hurry off when the group broke up, but Lyman caught him in the hallway.

"It was about Miss Carr, wasn't it?"

Rosenstone looked at him with barely concealed impatience. After a moment he answered. "Yes. She had an accident."

Lyman moved closer to him but didn't say anything.

Rosenstone rasped out a short, harsh breath. "She was found wandering on the Coast Highway last night, up around Topanga. Apparently disoriented."

"Where is she now?"

The doctor, clearly anxious to go, gave up his attempt at propriety. "Santa Monica Lutheran."

The rest of the evening Lyman mulled over what he knew of the story. And he remembered the warmth and emotion he had felt at that first meeting with Priscilla, Saturday morning, sitting with her in the kitchen. They had made a sort of pact to look to the future, and to help each other do that. It felt to Lyman like that had been more than a casual conversation. So he put aside his doubts and resolved to go see her the next day.

Since he was without an automobile, in the morning he called a cab company. He gave the man Doc Rosenstone's address.

"And where you going to?"

"Santa Monica Lutheran—"

"We don' go ta Santa Monica."

"I don't understand."

"We don't *go* out of town." The man spoke slowly, with emphasis, as if to a child. "We go all the way out there, we come back with an empty cab. Our driver loses money."

"Oh, well, I could pay more."

"We don't *go* there. That's what the train is for."

So Lyman asked the gardener to take him down to the Santa Monica Red Car. He assured the man, a solicitous sexagenarian with what to Lyman sounded like an Eastern European accent, that he would return long before the man went home at four o'clock. Not to worry.

It had been awhile since Lyman had ridden a streetcar, though God knows he had depended on them for an entire decade. In the thirties, people would ride the cars just for a place to sit down out of the sun or the rain or the smog, until the transit cops rousted them out. Now he noticed a certain prosperity that he had not seen back then, almost everyone with their face in a newspaper, and a few reading paperback novels—Lyman quickly scanned the covers of the books to see if any of them were his. No.

For Lyman today, though, the streetcar was not a refuge, but an escape. It had been weeks since he had been out roaming free in the world, and the feeling was invigorating and filled him with a kind of hope he had not felt for a very long time. He enjoyed the two-block stroll from the trolley stop to the hospital.

There was no patient listed as Pamela Carr, so Lyman asked for "Priscilla…"

"Tash?" said the woman at the desk.

"That's it," replied Lyman, hoping it was. "I only know her by her married name." That made no sense, but the woman gave him a room number.

Any exuberance he felt about being out in the world disappeared when he saw Priscilla. She had a scabbed-over scrape on her cheek and bandages covering parts of her arms and hands. But what disturbed Lyman was the acute pain and hollow despair in her face. She opened her eyes as he approached the bed.

"You found me," she whispered.

"Hi."

She nodded.

Lyman noticed another patient in the room, whose feet he could see beyond a portable screen. He wondered why she did not have a private room. That and the strange name, and the fact that Doc Rosenstone had not been able to find her for a night and a day. She was hiding again. "How are you?"

"Oh, not so good." She attempted to rouse herself. "I did something very foolish."

"Well, the important thing is that's over, and you can get better now."

Her forehead crinkled and tears dampened her cheeks. She turned her face away. He wanted to comfort her, to hug her, but of course any touch might hit a tender spot. "Try not to worry."

"The police said Kenny killed himself. That can't be true. I'm really afraid. He did it. I don't know how. I know he did. He had someone do it. He's as cold as a snake."

"Who is?"

"Morton. He can destroy people. And he killed Kenny. I don't know how. But he killed Kenny. Or he knows who did."

"Oh, I'm quite sure he doesn't."

"You don't know him."

Lyman searched for something else to talk about. Which somehow ended up being cats. She had left her beloved orange cat with Kenny when she moved out from New York, and he had left it with a friend when he came later. Now she wondered if she would ever see the cat again. Lyman had also abandoned a cat when Tina died. The housekeeper had taken him. He thought often of that cat when he woke up in the morning, The cat would usually come greet him first thing, expecting a lengthy head scratch.

A silly topic, but it was about a loss for each of them that would never be recovered. After awhile she drifted off. Lyman gazed at her sleeping, outwardly as beautiful and untroubled as a child. He saluted her silently and left.

By one o'clock, he was back in West Hollywood, sitting at a booth at Chasen's, the sort of "in" luncherie that Sheldrake loved and Lyman always avoided. But he was the guest, one might even say the guest of honor, at this celebration of his return to work. Lyman's sense of celebration, however, was sharply tempered by the very sad scene he had just come from.

And of course, the festivity was conducted without alcohol. He and Sheldrake drank coffee, but at the other tables there was enough liquor being thrown back to remind Lyman of all he would now be missing. He tried not to let it bother him, but it put him on edge.

Lyman soon found a distraction. A boisterous group at the back of the room made him turn around, and he saw Max Beckerman in the middle of a party that was conversing in French, German, and some other language. Was that Russian? Italian?

Max had introduced Lyman to the movie industry back in '43, in memorable fashion. They were both innocently involved in the scandal around the killing of talent agent Marty Nuco. They also, incidentally, wrote a screenplay—a protracted, acrimonious effort of two headstrong individuals, an experience from which Lyman was not sure he had yet recovered. But the movie Max directed from that script, *Double Down*, was still the best thing Lyman had worked on in Hollywood.

And they had parted ways on surprisingly friendly terms. Lyman had only seen him a few times since, but Max was always warm and even deferential to Lyman when they did bump into one another, perhaps because Max realized that a lot of the good stuff in that very good screenplay had come from Lyman.

Sheldrake was just paying the bill when Max approached the table, leading a striking young blonde woman, whom he introduced. Anna Something. She had a firm jaw, and brilliant blue eyes set above two gorgeous, dimpled cheeks. Sheldrake smiled and puffed up a little in the presence of the beautiful woman. Assuming they had come over to talk to Sheldrake, Lyman was surprised when Max turned toward him.

"And this gentleman here, is Mr. Wilbur, a great writer," said Max, smiling. Then he added some complicated German word that started with "Detective—."

"Very fine to meet you," said the woman. "Are you a detective? Or in the past?"

Lyman chuckled. "No, no. It's all in my imagination."

"Not quite," Max interrupted jovially. "This man once got me out of a terrible jam. And actually, some other people, too. He's a good one to know."

Lyman raised his hands in protest, but he saw a glimmer of interest or appraisal in the young woman's eyes, as if she had not expected to be introduced to a detective-gesundheit, or whatever that word was.

"Now." Max turned back to Sheldrake. "Now Fred, Anna is a terrific talent. She brings a, oh, I don't know, an exotic, a cool . . . excellent actress." He glanced at Anna. "You don't mind if I talk about you in front of your face, do you, dear?"

Anna smiled, uncomfortable but willing.

"She's just over," Max resumed with Sheldrake. "Papers all in order. She was in Germany, you know, so she knows about keeping papers in order." Max chuckled. No one else did. "She did some terrific things in Europe, just in the last couple of years."

Sheldrake smiled perfunctorily, just listening to a pitch now, like a hundred others he would probably hear this week from directors, producers, writers, actors, and probably even a set hand or script girl. His eyes fell to the check on the table, then returned to Max and the woman.

"She's signed with Blackwell, but they don't have anything for her now, so she's auditioning around. In fact, dear, didn't you say you were testing at our place for something this week"

"Yes," said Anna. "I have an appointment at Colosseum Wednesday, er, tomorrow, yes? I'm to see Mr. Arline?"

"So, Blackwell is shopping her." Max chuckled knowingly. "You know he always needs cash. And I'd love to have her for that next one I've got coming up."

Sheldrake wagged his head, a study in non-commitment. "Sure, sure. Ah, let's see. You're busy with that musical now."

"Just finishing up," said Max. "But Gabrilson is casting the spy movie. She'd be perfect for that. She can do good girl, she can do femme fatale."

"Fine." Sheldrake slipped a dollar bill onto the change tray before him and pocketed the check. "We'll see what's on the horizon. Give us a jingle later in the week. We'll see."

And having received an assurance that *we will see*, Max and the blonde headed back to their party.

This second mention of Morton Blackwell in a couple of hours gave Lyman a tingle. He had been sure that Priscilla, as he had now decided to continue calling her, had simply been hysterical with her accusations against the man. Two months ago Lyman only knew Morton Blackwell as a name, one of the poo-bahs of the movies. Then he had learned that Blackwell was producing the Alexander Stowbridge picture that he was interested in. Two hours ago, Priscilla had shown fear of Morton Blackwell as a kind of powerful and sinister assassin, and now here was a casual comment that painted him as a sort of pathetic character.

Sheldrake and Lyman walked to the front of the restaurant. "Good to have you back, my man." Sheldrake gave him a soft whack on the shoulder. "Make an appointment with Miss Sheffield. We'll see what we can get lined up for you."

"I know," said Lyman. "We'll see."

Sheldrake was oblivious to the joke. "No, we'll, you know… You're back on regular payroll. Back in the traces. Oh, by the way, we had your car towed to the Roosevelt Hotel. They're storing it for you."

"But I'm not at the Roosevelt. I never was."

"Well, okay. But your car is."

Anna

SHE HAD GONE to the lunch with Luguentz. It was a weekly informal gathering of the expatriate Germans and Austrians and other *mitteleuropeans* which consisted at any given week mostly of unemployed actors, writers and artists. They called themselves the Huddles, short for Huddled Masses, and they spent most of each get-together swerving between hope and cynicism. Some were unemployed because they were between pictures. Others, like Karl Luguentz were unemployed because they were just unemployable. He claimed that he deserved an associate director credit for a movie called *Lady from Shanghai* but had been robbed of this and blackballed because he had once been a communist. Now his long, dark visage could be found at all these meals, where usually the better-off ones would pick up his check. Anna had never heard of *Lady from Shanghai* or blackballs, but Luguentz had befriended Ferdie and her, and introduced them to the group. "Marlene shows up once in awhile," he had said.

After a couple of these lunches, Anna had trouble believing that Marlene Dietrich or anyone important would ever be involved with this group, but today Max Beckerman, the director, was not only there, he footed the entire bill. He was certainly one of the most important Germans in town, and one of the most charming, with sharply twinkling eyes and a ready wit.

That he worked at the very studio at which Anna was to have a screen test the next day was a coincidence, but it served as a natural opening to conversation when she might have otherwise sat at the table like a pile of straw.

At some point in a rambling conversation Beckerman realized he had in fact seen seen her first film, which was somewhat famous in Germany as the first commercial movie made after the end of the war. And this realization had led to him pulling her across the dining room to meet the producer from his studio. Max called it "table hopping," a funny phrase that Anna did not understand until he translated it.

And while meeting the producer, they had also, coincidentally, met Wilbur. That sequence of coincidences and meetings had caused her to think. It seemed like too many coincidences to be a coincidence. And it turned out that Mr. Wilbur was exactly the person she needed to meet. And he worked at Colosseum Studios. Where she had an audition coming up. She had been led to him for a reason.

Siegel had advised her to wait patiently for revenge on Morton Blackwell, like Dantès in *Der Graf von Monte Cristo*. But Anna was young, and her future in Hollywood uncertain. She did not want to wait patiently. Someone at the Huddles table earlier had talked about the actress who was having an affair with Morton Blackwell, whose husband had committed suicide—or did he? Everyone at the table seemed to know about this and to suspect dirty dealings that had to do with Blackwell.

When Max escorted her back to their own table, the party was breaking up, and she sat with him while he finished his coffee. At the other end of the table Luguentz was busy telling his story—the same story he always told about *Lady from Shanghai*—to Augie, a character actor who usually played the peasant, the servant, or the soldier who would be killed by a bomb. They paid no attention to Anna.

"Mr. Wilbur seems like an odd type to be a hard guy," Anna said to Max, as if just making conversation.

"Don't be fooled." Beckerman sipped the coffee. "Oh, he's a bit of a prig, as many who come from poverty seem to be. Lace-curtain Irish and all that. But he's been around. That's why I wanted him on *Double Down*—that's the script we did together. Because he knows high life and low life. And he has connections. He knows cops, and he knows guys who can get things done without too much concern for niceties."

He leaned toward her and in a low, confidential voice recounted the trouble he had been in and how Lyman had helped. Anna couldn't follow the whole monologue, but she understood that Beckerman had been wrongly accused of shooting someone and that Wilbur found proof of his innocence. And that Wilbur would stand up to bad men, and that he had connections with the police.

"He's a reformed drunk," said Beckerman. "Maybe that's where he gets his guts."

Priscilla

THE FIRST THING that happened was her mother came.

Dr. Rosenstone and Dr. Garman had had Priscilla released back to Doc Rosenstone's, where she could rest and be treated for the nervous breakdown brought on by the pressure of work and her husband's suicide. As they put it. Priscilla needed to get out of the hospital, so she was not in position to quibble about the exact reasons she had ended up there. She wasn't going back to the hotel that had been her seraglio, and most certainly not to Kenny's rented house.

So she was happy to go back to Doc Rosenstone's. That night her mama Jessie arrived and stayed with her daughter in the cottage. Priscilla had begun to recover, but her trials were not over.

There were arrangements to be made, things to be tended to, just the sorts of things her mother was so good at and that Priscilla could not face. Her mother, with the help of Mrs. Brown, from the studio, arranged to have movers go clean out the rented house and send most of Ken's things to Texas. And she had to face Morton, and her mother helped with that, too.

When he finally came to see her, Priscilla could tell Mort was surprised that Doc Robbie and her mother were in the room. This arrangement was important to Priscilla, though she did not tell anyone exactly why. Mort had to understand that he could only come to her as an employer, a mentor, a family friend, not as a lover. He seemed to grasp this right away, and she watched him quickly switch into that charming, humble man he could so easily be.

"Pamela, I'm sorry." Mort took her hand. "I'm shocked. We're all shocked. He was a very fine young man."

"You're very kind." She did not meet his eyes.

"Priscilla," said Mama Jessie. "Won't you introduce us?" She was obviously peeved that Morton had called her daughter Pamela.

"I was just about to, Mama. Mr. Blackwell, my mother, Jessie Tash."

Mort turned to the older woman and shook her hand. "A pleasure, at last."

She smiled and nodded, but Priscilla could tell she had something on her mind.

Doc Rosenstone entered the conversation. "It's a shame. So fickle is the flame of life."

"Indeed," said Mort. "Is there anything I can do? I know Mrs. Brown has been making arrangements."

"Yes," said Priscilla. "Please let her know how much I appreciate her help. We'll be catching the train in the morning." Priscilla and her mother were headed to Dallas, with Kenny's coffin in the baggage car. There they would be picked up and driven to Denton. "We'll be flying back. I'll be ready to go to work on Monday."

"Well, you look fine," said Mort.

"I'll be alright now." She could feel the doubt of everyone in the room. "My mother's going to be staying with me for a while. I have a cousin who lives in Glendale. We'll be staying there."

"I see," said Mort. "Okay. Don't get too far away."

"Oh, don't worry. It is Glendale, isn't it, Mama?"

Jessie shrugged and shook her head. She had something to say. "I'm very sorry to be so impolitic, but I find it difficult to sit here and pretend that you and my daughter were not engaging in an affair that started all this unhappiness."

Mort stood a little straighter. "I'm not going to lie to you Mrs. Tash—"

"And both married."

Mort said nothing. Priscilla's mother bowed her head as

if sorrow and contempt for the two of them was weighing her down.

"Mama, please, let's not discuss that now." Priscilla glanced at Doc Rosenstone.

"I'm sure you're aware, ma'am," said the doctor. "That your daughter and her husband had been estranged for some time. This is a difficult time for you, and for her, as it would be for anyone. Emotions run high, and it's natural to try to find someone to blame—"

"It's so comforting," Mama Jessie sniffed, "to have someone to explain everything."

Priscilla knew that she had to be careful about what she said next, but regret and self-loathing and helplessness were surging within her. "I'm grateful to Dr. Rosenstone for his help. This whole time has been so difficult for me, as Kenny and I grew apart. I don't want to blame him, but it has been . . ." She fixed her gaze downward. "I know what I have done, I know who's to blame."

She felt a movement, and looking up through tear-blurred eyes, she saw her mother coming toward her and kneeling to embrace her. They held each other motionless and silent for a long moment.

Anna

HER CALL WAS at seven o'clock the next morning. The movie, they explained to her, was about the last days before the war. In Paris, of course. The role was relatively small, a chanteuse at a cafe who meets the hero and has a brief but important conversation with him. And then the movie goes on and she has one more scene, really not more than a reaction shot. She would get to sing sixteen bars of a sad song full of regret.

After waiting several hours, she was called to do the scene a couple of times with a guy reading the part of the hero. She could sense, for really the first time since she had been in Hollywood, that the director or the producer or whoever was sitting there in the shadows had some real interest in her. The song had not been decided on, so they asked her to sing "Where or When," which she knew. A jolly-looking old Jew sat at a piano and kicked it off and she did the whole song.

Someone said thank you, and Anna looked around for the exit. Then someone said something she hadn't heard before. "Your agent is Rich Siegel? We'll be in touch with him."

A short slender boy in a sweater vest approached and indicated she should follow him. As they walked off the stage and headed down a passageway, she said. "I'm an old friend of Mr. Wilbur and I'd love to see him before I leave. Do you know where I can find him?"

The boy laughed. She could tell her beauty had an effect on him. "No, I don't. What does he do?"

"He's a writer."

The boy thought a moment. "Okay, wait." He walked back into the soundstage and was gone for several minutes.

When he returned he said, "Got it." He touched her elbow and opened a door, then followed her a few steps out onto the lot. "It's easy," he said. "That building there," he pointed. "Behind this one."

Anna nodded to show she understood.

"That's what they call the Producer's Building." He smiled and squinted. Sunlight reflected off his oiled hair. "I guess that's where the writers are. Anyway, that's what they told me. So head over there. You weren't pulling my leg were you? About knowing him? I don't want to get in trouble."

"No," said Anna. "Don't worry. But I won't tell anyone. Thank you very much."

"Sure," said the kid. He gave her one last appraising, almost regretful look and disappeared back into the soundstage.

Anna walked down the alley to the building he had pointed to, found a door and entered. She wandered through a hallway until she encountered the mail boy with his cart.

"Mr. Wilbur?" she said.

"Right down there," was the reply.

Again she went where directed. Her polite knock went unanswered. Rather than knock again she opened the door and peeped in. There was a man at a desk typing furiously from a notebook that was propped up next to the typewriter. The man was not Wilbur. But craning in a little farther, she saw another desk, and there he was, leaning back in a chair with his feet propped up on an open drawer, his eyes closed. She would have thought he was asleep except that the pipe in his mouth was puffing little balls of smoke into the air. She knocked on the open door, and both men looked toward her with no sign of recognition.

"Mr. Wilbur?"

His eyebrows went up.

"I'm sorry to intrude. I met you yesterday—"

He smiled. "At the lunch. Of course! Come in. You were

coming over for something today, a screen test or something, right?"

"Yes." Anna stepped into the room and shut the door behind her. "So I thought I would see if I could find you. And, well, I did."

"How did the test go?"

"Well, I think, but you never know."

Wilbur glanced at his office mate. "Well, it's good to see you again . . ." He had run out of words because he didn't know why she was there.

"I was hoping I could speak to you for a moment."

"Surely."

Anna glanced at the floor to avoid looking at him. "It's rather private."

"Oh. Well." Wilbur looked at the other man, who said nothing but whose expression and continued typing clearly meant *I'm not leaving.* Wilbur stood up. "Let's uh . . ."

He led her down the hall a few meters to where a small space opened up, just large enough for a receptionist's desk and a few chairs. The desk was abandoned and the little foyer empty of people. He indicated a chair for her, and then sat himself in the adjacent chair.

Anna let out a long, involuntary sigh. Her heart was fluttering. She had to go on—get this out. "Mr. Beckerman told me how you helped him once—"

Wilbur frowned. "I wish he hadn't said that."

"He told me more, and—" she hesitated. "I need to talk to someone about what I know."

"Are you in trouble?"

"No, not me. It's about Morton Blackwell. And the boy who died. I think he had something to do with it."

CHAPTER TEN
Thursday

Dr. Rosenstone

DOC ROSENSTONE HAD just finished the Thursday night group and come back to his office. He always remained in the office after group, to be available to any participant who wished to follow up on suggestions or interpretations from the session. And he left his door open to demonstrate that availability. As he wrote his notes from the session, Lyman Wilbur appeared ithe doorway. He stopped writing.

"Hi, Doc."

"Come in!" Rosenstone knew Wilbur had moved out a day or two earlier—not that he would necessarily have seen him around. The comings and goings and care and feeding of residents in the two bungalows out back and the three suites on the first floor were handled by the staff.

Wilbur sat in the chair across the desk from him. "I just wanted to . . . Miss Carr has left?"

"Yes, she went to Texas for her husband's funeral. Her mother went with her." Rosenstone cleared a bit of phlegm from his throat and wondered if the stuffiness he'd been feeling was going to turn into something bothersome.

"I saw her at the hospital the other day."

"Oh! Well." Rosenstone made a point of smiling. "She's still in a fragile state emotionally. I hope this trip isn't too much. I'm hoping the mother will provide some support."

"What exactly happened? I know you won't tell me anything confidential, but I have a reason to ask."

Rosenstone considered for a moment, weighing his curiosity against his ethics. "She had a nervous breakdown. That's a fancy way to say that she could no longer handle all the stresses in her life, added to the death of a cherished loved one."

"Cherished? Really?"

"People do not stop loving, defined as caring about and being deeply affected by, someone else just because they get divorced or separated. That can take years. Now, what is the reason for your curiosity?"

"Yeah." Wilbur glanced up at the ceiling, seeming to collect his thoughts. "She told me something, I'm wondering if she mentioned it to you. I don't want to, overstate it, you might say. But I thought I would talk to you."

Rosenstone had no idea what was coming next. He hoped it would not be about some unseemly and inappropriate attraction between the two.

Wilbur glanced up the ceiling again. "She seems to think that Morton Blackwell had something to do with the young man's death. What, exactly, she did not say. But she was quite fearful. Convinced. I brushed it off, but—"

Rosenstone found this interesting but not serious. "She is suffering from a lot of anxiety and regret. Obviously. So it doesn't really surprise me that she would say something like that."

"They are lovers?"

Rosenstone thought about how to phrase his reply.

"It's no secret," Wilbur prompted him.

"You heard this in group?"

Wilbur shrugged minutely. "I heard some things. But I'm back at the studio now. And there's no doubt that some of the talk there is just... anything that makes Morton Blackwell look bad will be repeated. Perhaps endlessly."

"Yes," Rosenstone reluctantly agreed. "They have a relationship. Pamela and her husband have been separated for a while."

"Yet she seems to fear him. Blackwell."

"Again, I wouldn't take a hysterical response to mean—"

"She was not hysterical. She was quite serious."

"Well, hysterical doesn't mean what you think it means."

"I see." Wilbur gave him an annoyed look. "But she is not the only one to tell me this. What I want to ask you is— you were there that night. Do you have any reason to suspect there was, shall we say, foul play?"

Rosenstone again weighed his ethical concerns against his curiosity. "Who told you that?"

"I'd rather not say."

"I don't know. The death was caused by pills and alcohol."

Wilbur leaned forward a little. "Yes, the *cause* of death was drugs and alcohol which stopped his breathing. What I'm concerned with is the *manner* of death, that is, what events in the few previous hours led to that extreme intoxication. That has not been determined, as far as I know. At least it hasn't been made public. I'm going to be talking to someone I know downtown. What I am asking is, did you see anything that made you wonder if this was not either an accidental or suicidal ingestion of the pills?"

Rosenstone studied Wilbur while he took a moment to formulate an answer. This was a side to the man he had only glimpsed before.

"Somebody downtown? You mean the police?"

"I do."

Rosenstone paused to consider. Was this a conduit he could use? And what would be the dangers of using it? Caution needed. "He obviously took the pills. He obviously had been drinking and should have known better. That's about all I can say."

"Do you know where the sleeping pills came from? How they happened to be there? What they were?"

"They were prescribed by a doctor. By his psychiatrist."

"Is this psychiatrist someone who is known to you? Is reputable—not some quack?"

Rosenstone let the word *quack* hang in the air for a moment. "She's well-known. Her name is Eloise Kness and she's a very qualified therapist, but she did give him a prescription for tranquilizers, which are easily abused. Only the patient controls the use—"

"Tranq—what?" said Wilbur. "I'm not familiar . . ."

"It's a new type of drug to relieve anxiety. They're not sleeping pills that knock you out. They are supposed to be relaxants, to relieve tension without the soporific effect. There's not a lot of history on them yet, which is why I advise patients to stay away. But some therapists, some doctors, are quite enthusiastic about them."

"And he was going to see this other psychiatrist, while his wife was in your care. Is that a common thing, that a husband and wife would each visit a different psychiatrist?"

"They weren't acting as husband and wife. Pamela was referred to me by someone at her studio. She was under a lot of pressure. She had been thrust into a very important and stressful role. Or position, you might say. I don't know anything about the history of Ken's treatment. I only know about him what Pamela told me."

"And you don't know of any reason why Miss Carr or anyone should fear Morton Blackwell?"

Rosenstone gave up the idea that Wilbur's tinpot "investigation" could somehow be used to stain Eloise. He had seen only hints of Wilbur's alter ego before, but now the private eye persona was in full flower. It showed evidence of continued recovery, certainly a good thing for him. After all, the man was a mystery writer. But the idea that he could be a conduit to police or prosecutors that would lead to anything useful seemed unlikely. "There are lots of reasons why people should fear him. Career reasons. But personally, physically, he is I'm sure, utterly harmless. Unless you're a starlet looking to be discovered."

Lyman

LYMAN'S RELATIONSHIP WITH LAPD Detective Will Henthorn was sociable but not close. They met when Henthorn was still a young cop holding down a boring desk job, hoping to be promoted. At the same time, Lyman had just started his career as a pulp-mag writer and cultivated connections with any policeman who had interesting things to tell him and was willing to talk. Henthorn seemed like he himself had aspirations to write, and follow in the footsteps of Deal Table, who had been a real detective and then virtually invented the hardboiled school of mystery.

Anyway, Henthorn was willing to talk to him back then when not many other cops or lawyers would. And they had maintained a sporadic but always cordial relationship since. Whenever they met they would quickly fall into a particular rhythm of conversation that went back decades. In fact, Will Henthorn's self-conscious but artful style of conversation had been something of a model for Lyman's written dialogue back when he was developing his style in pulp magazines.

The badinage applied whether they spoke in person, or, as in this case, over the phone. "So, Mr. Hollywood!" Henthorn would regale him. "How goes it?"

"Fair," Lyman would always reply. "No more than fair. Are you working the gutters this week, or the penthouses?"

After a few lines of such blather, a real conversation could be allowed. On this occasion Lyman asked, "Do you know anything about a guy named Kenny Preston?"

"As a matter of fact, his case landed on me. Not that I was looking for more work."

"It's a case?"

"Very definitely a case," said Henthorn. "I hope you

called me with information."

"All I have is rumor and innuendo."

"Spill."

"First—is Morton Blackwell at all in your interest in this?"

"Keep talking."

"That's a yes?" Lyman asked.

"Yes."

"May I ask why?"

"He was known to be screwing the guy's wife. That's always of interest. And Kenny Preston, per a source, was not known to be a drug user."

"I see."

"And Blackwell's alibi doesn't wash. He says he was home in bed. There isn't a worse alibi. You know that, Lyman. We haven't talked to his wife yet, but that doesn't matter. Wives. Worthless. All he has to do is come up with a legit alibi and we drop him. He bought gas, he passed a neighbor walking the dog. You know. Anything."

"But is he actually a suspect?"

"No," Henthorn growled, "Of course not. Until someone calls us and gives us a compelling motive, or puts him in the wrong place, or shows that he's lying, he doesn't need an alibi. Rich, powerful people don't bother killing the jilted husband. They don't need to. It just goes against everything in the entire Boston Blackie textbook."

Lyman wondered whether to proceed. He was of course not a trained policeman but a court jester, a troubadour, a spinner of popular tales.

Henthorn correctly read his moment of silence as a with-holding. "So, you called for a reason . . ."

"I've been told by someone that, that night, Morton Blackwell was in his office, got a particular phone call, became very upset and left abruptly. This was around eleven p.m."

"And who was this witness?"

"An actress. She was meeting with him."

"Meeting with him." The deadpan tone told Lyman that Henthorn suspected the meeting was of a prurient nature.

"I know. But she told me some details. Her husband took her to the meeting. She was admitted by a security guard. She described some details of the room."

"Then she needs to say these things to me. Not that I don't believe you, but, you know, the city pays me to talk to witnesses, though I appreciate you doing this pro bono work."

"But if she's telling the truth?"

"If she's telling the truth, Mort Blackwell may now need an alibi. A real alibi."

The Hollywood Star, Thursday, April 24

QUESTIONS IN DEATH OF YOUNG ACTOR
by Les Joseph

Early last Saturday morning police were called to a home on Garden Avenue in northeast Los Angeles. There they found a young man lying unconscious on the floor of a small unfurnished house. Kenneth Preston, 25, of Texas, was pronounced dead at the scene. According to a well-placed source, "the death was probably due to consumption of alcohol and sleeping pills, either accidental, or as a successful attempt at suicide."

But no evidence of intentional suicide was found, and an investigation by this reporter has turned up connections to a major filmtown mogul and a talked-about young actress.

The mogul is a producer and studio head, best known for a couple of very big hits a decade ago. The actress is a bright new discovery named Pamela Carr, who until recently was known as Priscilla Preston and was married to Kenneth Preston.

Ken Preston had been working in a New York production until a few weeks ago. Priscilla was signed to a contract by Blackwell Pictures last fall and came west in December to take on the title role in the film of the best-selling novel *Angeline*.

"Unfortunately for Ken Preston," said a source, "He discovered that his wife had also taken on a leading role in the profligate—in every sense—producer's affections." This well-known figure has been married to a member of another prominent movie-industry family for 13 years and the couple has two young sons. However, he is known in H-Town as a tireless philanderer who trades professional favors for sex. He had secreted Mrs. Preston in an out-of-the-way hotel during the film's production and rendezvoused with her there nightly. A source at the hotel confirmed that the producer "would often show up at Mrs. Preston's door as late as midnight and stay in her room for several hours."

However, it appears that Priscilla Preston may have grown tired of the constant and controlling presence of her lover.

The night Ken Preston died, Priscilla had gone into hiding, possibly with the intention of breaking off the illicit relationship. The suspected lover was in a frenzy trying to find her and may have visited Ken Preston's house late that night, possibly not long before the young actor was found dead, looking for Priscilla.

A confidential source in the Los Angeles County Coroner's Office says that the exact origin and nature of the drugs found in Preston's system have yet to be determined.

When asked to comment on the substance of this article, a spokesman for Blackwell Pictures refused to respond.

Mrs. Preston was reported to be bereft at he death of her husband. She is currently taking leave from the studio to settle the family's affairs.

CHAPTER ELEVEN

Friday-Saturday

Anna

HE WASN'T HARD to find. The person at the *Hollywood Star* gave Anna the number.

The phone rang. A voice said, "This's Joe."

"Les Joseph?" Anna asked.

"Yes, that's me. Among others."

Anna was put on guard. "What do you mean?"

"I have several pen names. You can just call me Joe."

"Very well. You are the one who wrote this story about Morton Blackwell and boy who died?"

"Yes. I wrote the story. I never said it was Morton Blackwell."

"Where did you get your information?"

"Who is this?"

"I think this story is about me."

"Really? Who are you?"

"I am the woman you need to talk to. You said he was in a frenzy. Well, I am the one who was there in his office. I heard him make the phone calls, and I know when he left."

"Go on."

"I told someone, and I think they told the police, and I think the police told you."

"I didn't get any information from the police, so I doubt it. But why don't you tell me your story?"

She told him the same thing she had told Lyman Wilbur:

how she had been called to the office, assumed it was some sort of audition; Blackwell on the phone, many calls. He was looking for a woman, Anna deduced, a particular woman who had gone missing or some such thing. And Blackwell said take *care of him* or *take care of it*. And she also heard something like *he'll be sorry*. Anna had not cared if Wilbur really believed her, or if she was caught in a lie. She hoped he would tell the police, and that someone would try to find the truth, that the right questions would be asked of Blackwell, and he would have to answer them. She wanted him to have to prove that he had nothing to do with the death of the young man, because the only way he could really prove it was to admit where he had been and what he was doing. Anna's strength was that she was his only true alibi.

She had given up on the hope that the law would act on its own against Blackwell or for her. It would be enough that he be forced to admit where he was at 11:15 Friday night, that he should have to say this in front of someone who represented authority, or decency or power. If a legal case came out of it, that would be fine, but not necessary.

When she had told Ferdie about what Blackwell had done to her, he had listened intently and held her when she needed to be held. Then she described how she could trap Blackwell. Ferdie was an engineer, a smart and worldly man. He told her, in a gentle and sweet way, that it was a crazy idea, that it would be the end of her career and possibly get her in legal trouble. He said they should talk to the police. Talk to a lawyer.

But the next day, he had changed his mind and wanted her to not only find an attorney, but to maybe try to talk to one of the gossip columnists. And when Ferdie brought home the *Star* with that story that very evening, she had to wonder if it was *her* story, if Lyman Wilbur had talked to the writer.

So she had called Joseph and repeated the story. When she was done, he again asked her, "What is your name?"

Anna had already decided about this. "I won't tell you now. Maybe later, if I trust you."

"Are you a U.S. citizen?"

"No. The fact that you are even asking."

"Where are you from?"

"Again, possibly later."

He paused, and Anna could tell by the sound of his breath that he was smoking a cigarette. He said, "And you were at his office, late at night, no one around. Your story does corroborate certain points." Another pause, another puff. "Alright. Now tell me again—the timeline of things is very important. When did you get there, to this office?"

"I had been told to be there at ten o'clock."

"Told by who?"

"When they called me that afternoon."

"Who called you?"

"Blackwell Studios."

"But who, specifically?"

Anna had been wondering that herself. Surely the woman who called her and set up the appointment knew the real purpose of the meeting, as much as the security guards did. "I don't know. I was at the reception desk at ten minutes 'til ten. There were two men there. Guards, yes? They made a telephone call and then sent me down the hall. I went into his office and he told me to sit down. He was on the phone."

"And then you just sat there. Could you hear what he said?"

"I could if I paid attention, but at first I didn't. I just watched the fire and wondered—"

"The fire?"

"Yes, the fireplace."

"In the office?" He chuckled, and his tone of voice when he spoke again was different. "Never mind. Of course. Was there also a waterfall?"

Her impatience grew. "I don't understand."

"Never mind. And when did he say these incriminating things?"

Anna wanted to make sure she got the timing right. "Right before he left. He left at eleven fifteen. I remember I looked at my watch."

"Kenny called me before eleven. When I got there about an hour later he was dead."

The change in tone and manner led Anna to believe that this man was now taking her seriously. "You were there?"

"Yes, he called me. I was the one who found him. He was my friend."

Anna was taken by surprise. "I'm sorry for you."

"Yeah, well. Have you talked to police?"

"I do not know who to talk to."

"Okay, tell me exactly what happened at eleven fifteen."

"That's when he just left. He didn't say anything to me. I suppose he forgot I was even in the room. I was sort of sitting in a corner, and it's a big office. He went out a door and did not come back. After about ten minutes, I left."

"So, about eleven twenty-five, eleven thirty."

"Yes."

"And the security men were still there?"

"That's right." May their souls burn in hell.

He paused again. Anna had reason now to think that he believed her.

"Alright, miss. I will look into this. Just give me your number."

"No, I will call you."

"You realize, depending on what I find, that you are not going to be able to hide for long. You will have to reveal yourself and tell your story to the authorities."

"Of course, that is what I want. But *you* realize that this will probably cost me any chance of ever working in films. And it may cost me even more. That is why you should believe me, and respect what I tell you. I have nothing to gain but everything to lose."

"Yes, I understand. I will do what I can to protect you, but you are probably right."

✧　✧　✧

ANNA WAS NOT hard to find either.

"Is this Anna?" asked the voice on the telephone, almost a lilting voice, like an Englishman. "I'm Lyman Wilbur. We spoke."

Now she remembered the voice. He was not English, just old, and old-fashioned.

"We need to meet," said Wilbur. He suggested the morning, since he didn't go to work until ten. She was unoccupied, so they agreed on a drugstore on Wilton Place, within walking distance of her apartment, and not far from the Colosseum gate. Anna assumed he was calling her for the same reason she called Les Joseph, because of the story in the *Star*.

But since she had talked to Joseph, she had begun to have a change of heart. Her anger had subsided. Blackwell had been exposed as a skunk, and suspicion had been cast on him. She did not know how Joseph got that information, but it accomplished her goal. And her ambition had returned, in the disguise of hopelessness.

She arrived at the drugstore. While waiting for Wilbur she walked the aisles of the small, clean, prosperous store, stopping at the magazine rack near the front window. There was displayed, on the covers of the various periodicals, the current state of the world. And there could be seen a world outside the movies, and performing, and her ambition. What if her career sank because of her need for revenge? What if she gained the justice she wanted but was fired by Blackwell and then no one else would have her? She knew of actresses

who had become involved in disputes or scandals in Hollywood who went to New York, to the theater world, and
succeeded. But for them it was almost always a return to a
safe and familiar place. That was not possible for Anna. In
front of her on the rack stood a copy of *Time* magazine
showing a Russian general, a cold-looking, ascetic man in
pince-nez glasses, a bald Himmler. She did not recognize the
name in the caption, but that was what else was happening in
the world. So where would she return to? Germany was
barely recovered three years after the end of the war, and
Berlin was now the center of political controversy between
the Soviet Union and the U.S. Her brother had written
describing how to get to Berlin one had to pass through the
communist sector, with the threat of being detained there.
The Russians were still in control but now had German
communists administering the country.

It would not be possible to ask Ferdie to go there, or
anywhere else. He had become her muse and support, and
was embarked on a career in the aircraft industry, which, like
movies, was based in Los Angeles.

She sat in one of the booths, still staring at the magazines.
Next to the commissar, an impossibly brilliant Rita Hay-
worth in a sun hat, yellow, orange and blue, red lips, pink
cheeks, blue sky, laughed at her. She could never be that,
either.

She was thinking of walking out when Wilbur slid into
the booth across from her, smiling, apologizing. After some
polite banter, he said, "There was a story that came out, in
the—"

"I know, I saw it."

"You saw it? Wasn't it about… I assumed the writer had
talked to you, and—"

"No," said Anna. "He didn't get any info from me for
that story."

"He didn't get that, what you told me, about the phone

calls and all that?"

"No, I don't know where he got his information."

"But it corroborates what you told me."

Anna did not understand that word, with robber in the middle. Doubt and fear overwhelmed her. Anna saw again the light of the gas fire glinting off his glasses, the damp feathers of hair that wobbled when he grabbed her and ripped her dress open. "He attacked me, and no one gives a—He attacked me but I got away, thank God. If he had pressed his flesh against my skin I couldn't stand it. I couldn't live with that memory."

Lyman stared at her as if at a lunatic. And why wouldn't he, after everything he had heard from her? She thought he would simply get up and leave, but he did not. He began asking her questions, in a quiet and understanding way, and she told him the truth.

Morton

MORT DEBATED, SOFA or desk? If he sat at the desk, it seemed like he could be a little more in control, on his throne, while the detective would be in the position of an applicant.

Which might be the best reason to not do it there, to not seem to be trying to power his way through the questioning. After all, he was innocent and had nothing to hide. The triangle involving Ken, Pamela, and himself was an affair of the heart. Mort had done nothing he had to apologize for, and there was nothing he could tell them about Pamela that could hurt her. Mrs. Brown, on Mort's behalf, had given her the weekend off. He hadn't seen her all that time. He had talked to Detective, or Sergeant, not sure, Henthorn on Tuesday and explained all this. The fact that Henthorn wanted to talk again indicated that Lyman could expect some tough questions. And that was before that unfounded and scurrilous story had come out in that rag. So even though he had done nothing wrong, Mort was worried. The interview was set for Friday at 10 a.m., a week after Ken Preston's death. His lawyer, Hester, would be present, just to keep things tidy.

On the sofa he could more easily act like what he actually was, an innocent man in a tough spot, hoping to receive a little understanding from the authorities. So the sofa it would be.

Except two detectives met him as he got out of his car at the covered parking space outside his private office entrance. Mort knew right away who they were. But they were over an hour early for the meeting, and who had let them in to wander around the premises? This was not a public area.

But they were cops, so they could do that. And Mort had nothing to hide.

"Mr. Blackwell, I'm Henthorn. We spoke. This's Greevey."

"Yes, we're meeting later, I guess." He closed the car door and was going to escort the men into his office, but Greevey leaned against the fender. "Or is this it?"

Henthorn smiled. "We'll be very quick, if you don't mind doing it now. I know you're a busy man."

Mort didn't try to move. Just get it over with. He didn't need his lawyer around to establish that he was innocent. There was not a shred of proof against him, because there could not be. "This's fine."

Henthorn was both a little rough looking and with his horn-rim glasses, a little smooth. "Let me explain the routine here. We have some very definite evidence about this death. But loose ends." He smiled again, "always the loose ends. I'm sure you understand."

Mort shrugged.

"You were having an affair with Mrs. Preston."

"Yes, of course."

"Had you ever met Mr. Preston, either before or, you know, after."

Mort knew he would do well to get used to innuendos about himself and Pamela. "I met both of them last fall. In New York. We signed her to a long-term contract and brought her out here in December. He was already working there, so he stayed."

"And then he came out here. Did you run into him?"

Mort assumed that Pamela had told the story of the confrontation in front of the hotel. "Yes. That was the only time I saw him since he came out. At her hotel. I was dropping her off. They had an argument."

"Were you involved in this argument?"

"Not really. It was him confronting her."

"He had discovered the affair."

Mort had already admitted this. It's not against the law to . . . "That was her free choice. I didn't have any claim on her. She could have gone with him if she wanted, and I would not have said a word."

"I see," said Henthorn. "Did he threaten you, or threaten her?"

Mort really wanted to move this into the office and started to turn that way, but again the two men remained planted. "No, but he wasn't happy. I really don't know what he might have said to her at any other time."

"Of course." Henthorn did the talking. Greevey wrote in a small notebook. "Now on the night he died, last Friday night, you told me the last time we talked that you were working in your office." Henthorn flicked his hand out. "This office right here?"

"Yes, do you want to go in?" Mort straightened up.

Henthorn did not try to stop Mort, but he also didn't move. "You were here until…?"

"I left just before eleven, I think. I went, I got in my car, and went home."

"Was there a problem with the phone?"

"The phone?"

"You said you were making calls. Did the phone work alright?"

Mort saw a glimpse of danger now and prepared himself. "The phone was okay."

"All the way through?"

"Yes."

"And you were alone here."

They had got to the blonde. "No, there was an actress who stopped in for a meeting. I'm not sure when."

"A meeting?"

"Yep. Some of my confreres like to go to nightclubs and do business. I do too, sometimes. But other times I have people come here. I can get a lot more done."

"Can you tell me her name?"

"Frankly, no. It's some kind of Russian alphabet soup."

Henthorn ran a thumb along his lower lip. "First name?"

"Sorry."

"How did the meeting go?"

"Fine. I decided to loan her out for a picture at another studio."

Henthorn smirked at him. "She's no Pamela . . . Carr, is it?"

"I don't know. Anybody could be anybody." This conversation had only been a few minutes, but it felt interminable.

"Well, the thing is, a source says that you left the office at eleven fifteen. Says you made threats on the phone and became very angry. Who were you threatening?"

Mort felt a spike of anger. "This is from that story in the *Star*. That is pure fiction. And possibly open to a libel charge. Look, I threaten people all the time. I don't murder them."

Henthorn was unmoved. "Who were you threatening?"

"I have no idea. She's either lying or exaggerating." Mort fought the urge to ask *why don't you ask her?*

"This would be the actress, that you don't remember the name, that you were interviewing and found a job for? Do I have that right? Why would she do that?"

"I have no idea."

"So what were you doing from eleven fifteen on? There's no record of phone calls after that time."

Mort wondered if that was really true. He couldn't afford to assume it wasn't. "Business. I don't know. If it wasn't phone calls it was memos. Honestly, I can't say."

"So you were in this office. Working."

"If she says I wasn't, she's lying."

"Actually, *you* said that, just a minute ago, that you left at eleven."

"I said approximate. I can't swear either way."

Now Henthorn pulled his own notebook out of his jacket pocket and studied something there. Without looking up he said, "So whaddya think, Mike?"

Greevey sighed and reached out as if was going to pat Mort on the shoulder. But then he dropped his hand. He said, "Look, Mr. Blackwell, we know you didn't kill Kenny Preston. But you were his wife's lover, and he may have been murdered, and I need some definite information from you. Then we walk away and you never see us again."

"Fine."

"So. Eleven o'clock hour."

"I was with the girl."

"Thank you," said Mike. "Now that wasn't so hard, was it. You have sex?"

Mort nodded.

Henthorn said, "She says you raped her."

Mort felt relieved. He could get through this. "No, God, no."

"But you got a little over-excited."

"What do you mean?"

Henthorn slid the notebook back into his pocket. "You ripped her dress off her."

"I don't remember that. It was a passionate encounter."

"Wham bam thank you—"

Mort cut him off. "Don't get crude. She comes in, throws herself at me, she's beautiful. I'm not made of concrete."

"So you were here, having sex, consent debatable, until eleven thirty."

Mort considered all options, all routes. Where to stand, when to give up.

Henthorn scowled at him. "So you were here having—"

"Yes. Yes."

"And then you went home."

"Uh huh. Yeah."

"Alright." They looked at one another, sharing the same smug expression. "That's what I need to hear," said Henthorn. "As far as Kenny Preston."

"Good."

"But the girl says she did not consent, and that's rape or assault. And I have your denial. Someone else may come talk to you about that." He glanced at Greevey. "We have other fish to fry."

Act 2 Curtain

CHAPTER TWELVE
May

Lyman

"I TALKED TO Stowbridge about you," said Fred Sheldrake.

"Yeah?" Lyman had just walked into the office. He took a seat.

"He saw your real estate movie. Really liked it."

"*Due at Closing?*" Lyman was dismayed. "That's nothing. I wish he'd—"

"He saw some others, but that's the one he mentioned."

Lyman had not known this was happening. Of course he would want Stowbridge to see *Double Down* or at least *The Stars Above Us*, but not *Closing*, which was a sin-in-the-suburbs potboiler, a B-shot all the way. "He probably likes the parts Mowry wrote. Oh, well."

"The point is, he liked it." Sheldrake was never a patient man. "You're probably not the best judge of your own work."

"In this case, I hope not. But why was Stowbridge talking to you? I thought Blackwell was doing that one."

"We're partnering. He's short of money, but he's got Marte Lindgren." Sheldrake smiled around his unlit cigar. "She's in this. And then we get her for our own picture."

Lyman shook his head at the producer's obvious gloating. "Flesh peddlers."

"So," he continued, "the Stowbridge movie has this psychiatrist in it, and I didn't tell Stowbridge this, but I know you've been in therapy, and I thought, y'know, you could give it a fresh angle. And since we're now producing, if you end up doing the screenplay, you just stay on our payroll." Sheldrake paused for effect and took a long moment to light his cigar. Lyman wondered what was coming.

"They want you to do a treatment. It's a foot in the door."

"Well, God damn it!" Lyman couldn't help chortling.

Sheldrake held up a book in a blue cover. "Read the book, write ten or twenty pages of a plot and character summary."

Lyman felt a flush much like victory. It hardly mattered who this *they* was who wanted him. He was being given a chance to take a whack at it. It had been partly just to get this opportunity that Lyman had dried out and started seeing Doc Robby. A treatment was, like the man said, a sketch, an outline of an outline. But if they liked it, they might have him do the screenplay. "Now that would be something."

"Be careful what you wish for," said Sheldrake. "Blackwell is the producer. He and Alexander Stowbridge are two of the champeen assholes around. They're both arrogant, egotistical, they think they know everything. Of course they can't *both* know everything but, like I said, ego. I'm surprised one of them hasn't murdered the other. But they've done three pictures together, so . . ."

"No kidding." The tossed-off reference to murder gave Lyman a little pause. Of course, Sheldrake did not know about Lyman's glancing involvement with Priscilla Preston, or his conversations with Anna Andrzejewski. After Anna confessed to him that she was lying about Mort, Lyman took her to see Henthorn, who not only had utterly believed her, he had cursed Mort Blackwell.

Sheldrake leaned back and crossed a leg over a knee. "How do you feel about the head-shrinky stuff?"

"Every story I've ever written was about a psychopath.

Cold-blooded murder is as inhuman as a human can get."

Mentioning *every story* gave Lyman another internal pause. Almost every story he had ever written, good or bad, had been done with Tina sitting in the other chair, or lying in the other room, or waiting at home. The furnishings of those rooms, those homes, had gone during the course of their life together from stylish to threadbare and back to plush. But she was always in his life, in his rooms.

He had finally gone out to the house and done all the necessary chores of moving out and putting it up for sale. He was able to get rid of most of the stuff to a used furniture man and stored the rest at Bekins. He gave them five years rent in advance, expecting he would never go there again. The man who took the money never blinked, and it occurred to Lyman that people-never-coming-back was a pretty common thing in that business.

The Sunset Tower also held memories, alcoholic regretful ones, and he didn't want to go there either. So he moved into one of the new seaside apartments in Playa del Rey. It was a drive, Culver Blvd. to Venice Blvd. to Fairfax to Melrose, but Lyman usually compensated by leaving for work after ten in the morning and staying until late in the evening. He had nothing to do at night anyway except to read and write. In the mornings before work he would sometimes walk down on the beach, never too near the water, and soak up the sun, or the chill wind, or the fog. Didn't much matter which it was.

One of the things he thought about as he walked was the life, rather than the death, of Kenny Preston. He thought he could feel the despair that Kenny felt. Lyman had once been an ambitious, headstrong, volatile young man. Once he found Tina, he found many other things. And Tina had never given him reason to doubt. But how would he have felt, and what would he have done, if she had turned her back on him? He was already a borderline reprobate, a drinker, a malcontent. To have absorbed that loss would have left him feeling as hopeless as he now felt, but boiling over with and energy that would undoubtedly have been expressed as anger and self-loathing.

How lucky he was that at Ken's age, he had never had to deal with a loss like that.

Priscilla

SHE CAME BACK from Texas with a resolve: She was going to marry Mort and enjoy wild success in life and in her career.

Sometimes she was going to do that. The rest of the time she was going to enter a convent and try to find absolution for her sins against Kenny and against every ideal she had ever cherished.

"But it wasn't the way you might think," she told Doc Robbie. "When I was there, with Ken's family, is not when I felt guilty. They were so generous and so sweet. They didn't show any resentment or anger. They could see I was suffering. Even his parents, who were dealing with their own sadness, they just embraced me, even though I have always known they didn't want him to marry me."

"That's when I felt like, by God I'm going to succeed, I'm going to knock 'em dead in whatever I do and become a star, just like Kenny and I used to talk about when we were first together. I'm going to justify his faith in me and make those dreams come true."

She stopped talking, feeling the pull of emotions, remembering the soapy floral scent of Ken's mother when they hugged, and the brave, pained look on the older woman's face. Mrs. Preston and Mrs. Preston . . .

Dr. Rosenstone said, "And when do you feel the hopeless feeling?"

"When I'm alone."

"But your mother is with you now. Is that difficult?"

"Oh yes, but it's also something I need. She's a wall I can hide behind."

Priscilla felt like the doc knew what she was talking about. Sometimes psychoanalysis was frustrating that way. It wasn't a conversation: it was a monologue for an audience of one. "You know how it is with Mort. Yes, a wall is what I need. And here's where it comes together. I know I was wrong to have an affaior with him. And wrong to be unfaithful to Ken. Now I am going to start doing right. If he wants me, marry me. Or get the hell off my plantation."

She had never felt ashamed about the affair while it was going on. Even now she didn't feel shame. Guilt, yes, along with what she kept thinking of as resolve. If Mort wanted her, that would be how they would do it. If he didn't want her, she would be alone. She felt like she deserved to be alone and thought about something Lyman Wilbur had said about cherishing his solitude. Being alone she could be with Ken. Yes, life would go on, but she wanted always to be able to have moments alone with him.

And whether Mort married her or not, she was resolved that his energies would be focused on her career. She had just spent a half a year living inside a complex historical character who was devoted to God but expressed that devotion by living a unique and powerful personal life, by defying convention and authority. That portrayal, Mort and others had told her, was going to make Mort more wealthy and powerful than ever. And Priscilla, as Pamela, wanted some of that wealth and power.

Indeed, the very creation of Pamela Carr had sealed that promise. Pamela was a combination of Priscilla's talent and Mort's direction. Priscilla had given up her life, and had destroyed Ken, in the name of Pamela Carr, who looked like Priscilla, and whose voice sounded identical. But Pamela Carr was coldly calculating, strong-willed, shrewd, and devoted to her own goals.

Now Mort would have to show a similar focus on her career. He had the means to do it, the connections, and the energy of an atomic chain reaction. But he had lacked focus, and she would help him with that by cajoling and demanding that the focus be on her. Priscilla could never have pulled that off. But she knew Pamela could.

Half the time.

Doc Robbie said, "And your mother gives you the strength, or the authority, to confront Mort?"

"Yes, absolutely. Just as a puzzle he has to solve, sort of. I live with her. She watches where I go, who with, and when I come back. It's like being in high school again, except this time I don't resent it."

"Back before you met Ken."

Priscilla felt that needle, in her gut. "Yes, of course."

"So would you say this is also a way for you to cope with that loss?"

"I guess so. When I was with Ken, he was the most important person in my life. But he was equally committed to me. I can never have him in my life again, but I can carry that love that we had. I carry it everywhere I go. If Mort wants to serve that love, I will give him all I can. But that personal devotion Ken and I shared only exists in two places now. Half of it is working for my career. The other half is locked in his grave."

Anna

THEY WENT TO the art museum, their second or third one. Anna marveled at how the museums of Los Angeles seemed to contain all the wonders of art and culture from the ravaged continent she had recently left. For fifteen minutes she gazed in wonder at a portrait by a Dutch artist of a young woman whose luminous eyes and pale eggshell face looked back at Anna across centuries. It seemed impossible that that world had ever existed. And surely that painting, if it had remained in Amsterdam or Cologne, would have been destroyed or stolen.

The museum they went to was on a street of fancy shops. It was Sunday, so they had plenty of time to laze, and they were strolling to a late lunch. Anna stopped to look into the window of a jewelry store. It was strictly an exercise in fantasy to look at jewels. She was now on a six-week loan-out to Colosseum, though not on the picture she had auditioned for. But whatever the case, she was making more money than she ever had, although she recognized that to say that was silly since she was still only twenty years old. But she was happy to be able to send most of that money to her family in Frankfurt.

She and Ferdie could easily live on the salary from his engineering job, but two weeks prior, the union at the aircraft plant had gone on strike. Though Ferdie was not a member of the union, he and the rest of the technical staff had been advised not to cross the picket line. So her salary would help. They couldn't afford to buy a diamond brosche today, but they could look. And then she could buy him lunch.

Anna was turning back toward the sidewalk when a well-dressed woman and man approached her. The man wore sunglasses and a jaunty smile and it took Anna a moment to recognize him. It was Morton Blackwell.

Before she could react, Blackwell grabbed her hand and lifted it. Anna had a delirious feeling he was going to kiss it.

"Here she is!" He patted the back of her hand and half turned to the woman he was with. "Miss Andrez-ewski." The woman, who had to be his wife, took the hand and shook it, and then Anna got it back.

"How's it going on the production?" asked Blackwell. He was wearing an iridescent light-blue jacket, and seemed as tanned as if he lived on a beach.

Anna mumbled some stupid but polite answer.

"Terrific!" Blackwell smiled, and the woman, who had dark, golden hair, grinned and nodded happily. Then they were gone, and Anna looked at Ferdie, who had never turned around, but had watched the whole exchange in the reflection of the store window.

✧   ✧   ✧

ON MONDAY MORNING Anna was on the set for the second week of the shoot, still happily but cautiously getting used to things. Show business is show business, but she had much to learn about Hollywood studio ways.

She was playing the "Swedish Girl" in a drama based on a book called *The Jungle*. To help improve her English, and to learn more about the role, Anna had got a copy of the novel by Upton Sinclair and had begun to go through it. She identified strongly with the characters and their difficulties in a harsh, authoritarian society, but the movie was much more bland than the book and focused on the love story of the two main characters. The star of the show was Joan Gilbert, an established star at Colosseum. Anna's role was secondary.

After hearing her name mispronounced repeatedly, she

had agreed to be billed as Anna Amelia, in honor of her late friend from UFW. This was one aspect of her new resolve to put aside her troubles, to push through—again—the unsavory and corrupt aspects of show business and simply do what she must to succeed. Amalia would never have that chance.

Anna became aware that there was an unexpected delay. The shot had been set up, but the director had yet to appear. The actors and crew were standing in small groups and relaxed poses, just waiting. Anna, with nothing to do and no one to talk to, read ahead in her copy of the script even though she had already been through it a dozen times or more.

There was a stir, and the director, MacKay, walked in. "Miss Amelia," he called, striding over to the offstage makeup table. He glanced at her, obviously peeved, and Anna wondered what unwritten rule or custom she had broken. "Have a seat," he said, then barked over his shoulder. "Mrs. Landers!"

The makeup artist appeared, and the two of them studied Anna's face, consulting together in a verbal shorthand that Anna did not understand. Suddenly Morton Blackwell was leaning into the nestle, growling in his impatient baritone. The makeup lady dampened a cloth and began to wipe Anna's face.

"Sorry, dear," she muttered, making brief eye contact. Then she was plucking Anna's eyebrows, painting and brushing her cheeks and nose and chin.

Sitting there helpless, Anna darted looks around the set, which had felt relaxed and friendly a moment before, but now seemed clouded with mixed tension and disgust. She wondered what had happened and why Blackwell was here. She had wanted to destroy him, and at one point had even been willing to sacrifice her Hollywood career to do that. But since starting this film, and experiencing the everyday brilliance of almost everyone involved in the filmmaking process, her hunger to be here, to succeed here, had returned.

And now, for no reason that she could see, Morton Blackwell was everywhere in her life.

"There," said Landers, and she turned to MacKay, who turned to Blackwell.

"Good!" said Blackwell. "Much better." He clapped MacKay around the shoulders. "I'm not here just to be an SOB. Just keeping an eye on my filly. She's very important to me. I'm sure you understand."

"We want to cooperate," said the director, relieved that he would soon be rid of the interloper.

Anna stood up, wanting very much to just fade into the background, still confused. Mort turned and surveyed the soundstage. He spied Jo Gilbert watching these proceedings from a seat at the edge of the lighting. "Watch out for her," he fairly called, pointing at Anna. "I caught her yesterday shopping for diamonds in Beverly Hills." He shook his head and chuckled. "Watch out for her." He turned back to Anna. "If there's anything you need, young lady, you have my number."

Then he was gone, and Anna knew why he had been there. It was a message. *I will forgive you your indiscretion, but I am in control. Don't challenge me or you'll be on the first ship out.*

From that day on, everyone in the building looked at Anna differently—whether out of respect or resentment hardly mattered. The welcoming and openness she'd been treated with was replaced by a sort of professional indifference.

But Anna had not come this far to make friends.

❖   ❖   ❖

THEY SAT BY the train all afternoon and into the evening. The crowd of passengers slowly thinned as some people walked down to a nearby highway hoping to catch a ride on a passing car or truck that would allow them to further their journey, or at least get to a place where they could find shelter and some food. But the film crew—some twenty-five people with trunks of equipment—was stuck. They were either going on to Salzburg or back to Berlin. Around midnight, there was some light and noise at the rear of the train. Everybody who was left climbed back on and the train went in the opposite direction for awhile. The conductor came through and told them they were returning to Nürn-burg and then would resume the trip south over a different route.

Assured of their eventual delivery, most of the passengers slumped over or leaned back and closed their eyes. Anna fell into a restless sleep, dreams replaced by bumps and jostles and abrupt stops, followed by starts so slow you could not tell the train was moving. She was too tired to care much about what was happening. It was out of her control.

In the gray early light she woke again. Amalia was sitting, staring out the window. Anna lifted her head and saw farm fields and distant clouds. "Where do you think we are?"

"I saw a sign that said Augsburg," Amalia whispered hopefully.

"Oh."

She fell back asleep, but the sound of the airplanes jolted her awake. It was full sunlight now, and the howl of the fighters shook the very air. The smoke from the engine was blowing in through the windows as the train shuddered forward, the cars rocking on their wheels. A huge deafening explosion seemed to lift the train into the air, where it hung for a moment before it slammed to the ground and lurched over onto its side. Anna clung to the arms and backs of the seats, as dust and smoke and leaves—she would always remember the leaves—blew into her face, choking her. A sudden backward jolt tore loose her grip and she hurtled against something, a bar or rail, that caught her under the ribs and smashed the breath out of her.

Then everything stopped.

When Anna found Amalia she was slumped face down in the dirt beside a tree stump. She looked like she was trying to get up. But she did not get up, because her skull had been smashed in and she was dead.

Morton

TO CELEBRATE THE wrap on *Angeline*, Mort had gone on a weekend gambling spree in Tijuana, lost money, drank too much, ate too much. But he couldn't afford to have a hangover so he banished the very idea from his mind. He had important meetings all day for the start of *The Stowbridge*, as the movie was called at the moment, since no other title had stuck.

The least important of these meetings was this one with Stowbridge himself, Wilbur the mystery writer, and the psychiatrist. This would be about the script. The other meetings were about getting the picture financed and scheduled, necessities without which a script would not matter.

The door from Mrs. B.'s adjacent office opened, and she walked in holding a notepad. She was the only person who could come in without going through the receptionist. "Sullivan called," she said. "No offer yet. We need to talk about some of these numbers."

"Okay," said Mort. Sullivan's clients would be the second option. That was studio holding-company money, and it was expensive.

"And the banker—" Mrs. B. continued, but she was interrupted by the buzzer as the door from reception opened, and there stood Lyman Wilbur, blinking uncomfortably. He looked somewhat like a detective with his frumpy tweed suit and darting eyes.

Introductions were made and the three of them stepped over to the parlor, as Mort thought of it, the seating area around the gas log, which was turned off.

As they sat, Wilbur said, "You've finished the Angeline

movie. That must be a relief."

Mort wondered what exactly he was referring to. "Yes, it is."

Wilbur ducked his head a little. "I know Miss Carr. We have the same psychiatrist. We happened to run into each other."

Pamela kept surprising Mort in unpleasant ways. And now she had some kind of relationship with this guy? He offered a bland smile. "Dr. Rosenstone has helped her immensely in the aftermath of her husband's death."

"It seems so," said Wilbur. "The little I've seen her."

"I can vouch for that," said Mrs. Brown. "She's getting along well."

"It's pretty sad," continued Wilbur. "A young man, with some talent, I hear."

Mort wondered why they were discussing this. "We were actually about to give him a contract. But he was unfortunately not ready for—"

Mrs. B. interrupted. "He was unstable. Maybe even dangerous."

"—but he had already burned those bridges by the time he. . . ."

"And his end tables," said Mrs. B., with a smirk.

Mort felt like he had missed something. Mrs. B. could be inscrutable, and even a little threatening herself. The door buzzed again and Stowbridge entered with a stocky woman in a dark silk brocade dress that almost reached her ankles. The psychiatrist. Eloise Kness. More introductions made, seats taken again. Mort got right to business. To Lyman: "We read your treatment. What did you think of the book?"

"Not much. It does have possibilities, though."

"It's got characters," said Stowbridge, his dark eyebrows climbing halfway up his broad, smooth forehead. "And one interesting twist. That's probably all we need from it."

"Yes," said Mort. "So we liked your ideas. We already

had a completed screenplay."

Wilbur frowned briefly. "I didn't know that."

"That we don't like. Well—" Mort glanced at Stowbridge. "—Alexander thought it was serviceable. Anyway, we'd like you to take that script, add your ideas and your style. You have a distinctive way with the characters."

"He's the king of the evil housewife," Stowbridge chortled.

Wilbur smiled at this cryptic compliment. "Well, thanks for noticing. I take care with my female characters. Especially the more unassuming ones."

"And speaking of unassuming women?" said Stowbridge.

Mort nodded. "Yes. So the one weakness I see is, none of the versions are very up to date on the psychology angle. and that's where Dr. Kness comes in." He faced her. "She's read your treatment. What did you think, madam—er, Doctor?"

Kness sat up in the chair so that her feet reached the floor. "A brilliant story, without a doubt." She shared a warm smile with everyone in the room. "But as you said, the psychological aspects are almost medieval."

Mort caught a passing look of consternation on Wilbur's face. No one else seemed to see it.

"But that's easily rectified. It's mostly language. Terminology. Your psychiatrists have to have the modern lingo."

"I see," said Mort.

"And awareness of the symbols. For example, the scene of flying in a curvy airplane is full of symbolism." Doctor Kness smiled impishly. "An erection of the penis. And when they land, female masturbation."

A brief silence in the room was broken by Stowbridge.

"I say!" he muttered softly, his eyes twinkling under those stiff, dark eyebrows.

CHAPTER THIRTEEN

June

Lyman

THEY HAD NOT told him the schedule until the end of the meeting. Six weeks would be a challenge. But they also did not say that there would be almost daily meetings about the script, and that both Mort, more often, and Stowbridge, less frequently, would lob new ideas and twists at him that he would have to at least consider, argue against, or massage into the script. The mental effort required made the process seem like slogging through deep, sticky mud.

They also had not told him that bringing in the psychiatrist had been entirely Mort's idea. He learned this from Stowbridge, who made it clear in their private meetings that he already had plenty of his own ideas for the film and that he was going to incorporate at least some of these, no matter what Lyman put in the screenplay.

But because of the meetings he saw Priscilla again. She was in the Blackwell Studios parking lot, headed out, when he was walking in. She said she was off for another week, then starting a loan-out at Paramount. Lyman hadn't talked to her since she was in the hospital. She looked much better now, of course.

"So that's me," she said. "Why are you here?"

"I'm on loan-out, too. Here."

She shook her head. "What a world!"

"Yes, here we meet, two debentures passing in the night."

She laughed brightly. "Yes, here we are." She was about to walk away but stopped herself. "Doc Rosenstone told me about . . .or not about . . . but that, you helped make the police understand."

Lyman felt that his role in clearing Mort Blackwell should remain as little-known as possible. For one thing, he hadn't done that much. "I had a small part to play. A coincidental meeting. I helped put the right people together. Dr. Rosenstone was helpful in that."

"Well, thank you. I feel like I was a little hysterical."

"You had had an awful shock."

She sighed, and Lyman could see the beginning of a tear in the corner of her eye.

"It's made me tougher," she said. She shook the pain away. "But my mama has been staying with me. That has helped." She reached out to grip his fingers gently. "And friends."

"I'm sure you have much better friends."

"I'm lucky. Carla has been a rock for me."

"Is that the lady from the studio? Blackwell's assistant?"

"Yes, Mrs. Brown, everyone calls her all the time. Out of respect. She's his secret weapon. And the Mother Superior. When I was at my worst, with no one to turn to, she would take me home with her sometimes, and we'd have dinner with her son, and play a game, or listen to the radio. Then she'd make me a cup of herb tea and tuck me in. Those were the only nights I could relax and not worry."

"Well," said Lyman. "As they say, when the going gets tough, the tough lie down."

She laughed. "You are funny. You should be on radio. But I just realized why you're here. You're writing Morton's new picture."

"Well, I'm trying."

"I know, I know," she said. "He can be a meat grinder."

Anna

THROUGH THE HUDDLED Masses, Anna had indeed met Marlene when she showed up for lunch unannounced one day. While Max Beckerman had commanded the table through his ebullient personality, Marlene seemed to draw every eye through some sort of electromagnetic force. She did not pay everyone's bill, but she invited Anna to tea the following Sunday.

It was a revelation.

Of the seven women there in Marlene's formal dining room, Anna thought she recognized a couple of faces, but she could not attach them to names. Two were Marlene's age or older, the others closer to Anna's age. Only one, besides Marlene and Anna, spoke with an accent, possibly English or Australian. What they all had in common was that each of them knew a famous, or powerful, or brilliant movie man who was—

"A pig!" said the redhead with green eyes. "What a pig is to a pig is what he is."

"A disgusting toad," said Joanna, the brunette with high cheekbones.

"Crawled out of the sewer," said Abby, who was at least fifty years old.

And they had each had unwanted sex with the disgusting creature they were describing, who included the head of production of 20th Century Fox, the top male box-office draw of 1938, a former famous child actor, and Louis B. Mayer's hatchet man. Some of the names didn't mean anything to Anna, some were among the most famous names in the world. And all of them were still dancing through their days, untouched, unashamed. Except Abby's pig, who had later died of a stroke. "He brought me up to his room from a party at the Biltmore. I'd gotten plastered on champagne. I was so drunk I peed in the bed. *He* was so drunk he never knew it. Thank God he didn't get off. I'd hate to have had to get an abortion. But I would've. Believe me."

Anna was confused. "He didn't get off? How did you get away?"

Abby grinned. "No." She struck a fist into the palm of her other hand and shot it out in front of her, *"Get off."* It looked to Anna like a kind of Nazi salute. But all the women cackled, and Anna understood.

Louise, one of the younger ones, was just as tough. "Trapped me on his boat. The servant disappeared and we did it all day. At first I fought him, but it didn't do any good. So I just figured he owed me, and I kept counting. From the second I said *no* and he kept going, the meter was running."

"Did he pay?" asked Terry, the dyed blonde.

"You know he did. His agent got me second lead in *The Fury*. And then he got me a seven-year kay with Paramount." Anna later learned that *"kay"* was short for contract. And the long-term personal services kay with a major studio was the gold standard.

There were more stories of drunken grabbing, of weight pressing you down, of career or personal extortion. And what the women all shared was the feeling of being trapped, in danger, under heavy duress. If there was a difference between these men in their expensive cars and clothes and homes, and the brutal, uneducated, unwashed Cossacks who had stormed into Berlin, Anna felt that at least the soldiers took what they wanted and then left you alone. But here, you had to live around them, work around them. The stories went on and on for what must have been an hour, and for the first time since her attack Anna felt she was in a place where she could tell her story and be believed, and beyond that, *understood.*

So finally she did tell it. The nods and expressions of

disgust included her into the group. Marlene did not tell a story of her own, and Anna was mystified. How had she known to invite Anna to meet these women? What had marked her?

"Because of where you work," Marlene told her later. "At Blackwell." That was all she said, and all she had to say. And how had she found the other women? "In fact," said Marlene, "they weren't that hard to find. They are like driftwood on the beach after a storm."

✧ ✧ ✧

FERDIE, TEMPORARILY UNEMPLOYED, had gone to play poker with his fellow fugitives from the working life. Anna was about to get ready for bed when the phone rang.

"Anna?"

"Yes."

"This's Joe Gianelli—Les Josephs. We spoke—"

"Yes." Anna had a flash of fear—or excitement. For him to be calling her now could only be trouble of some kind. "How did you get my name?"

"Oh." He chuckled. "I'm a reporter. I got your number from your call to the *Star*. I have since learned that you were not truthful with me, and I have reason to be upset with you." But he sounded more teasing than angry.

"You never printed what I told you."

"No, I didn't. I wrote something, but there was no way to corroborate it. Good thing, cuz I'm in trouble enough for the first story, the one I assume you read."

"But you said that Blackwell was involved in the boy's death. Was that not true?"

"I think it might be." He sounded apologetic. "Obviously the source I had for the story was not reliable. But I know there was a germ of truth to it. But anyway, I'm calling to see if you have had any problems."

"Problems?"

"From Blackwell or any of his hirelings. He has a whole football team of double-dealers and fixers."

Anna considered what might be going on here. She decided to tread carefully. "No. No problems."

There was an odd silence on the line for just a few seconds, and then the voice said, "You too?"

"I beg your pardon?"

"I don't blame you."

"I'm sorry, I don't—"

"I've been blackballed. No one wants to talk to me now. It's really pretty funny," he said in a sorrowful voice.

"Because of that story?"

"Of course, that story," said Joe. "I reached too far. But there's a seed of truth in that story. I just couldn't figure it out. I screwed up, but there was a seed of truth there. You see, I know someone was there at Kenny's house that night. I thought it might have been Blackwell, but I can't prove that."

"I remember you told me you were there, the night he died."

"I was the one who found him."

A little prickle of excitement pattered across her scalp. "But there was no one else there?"

"No, but I know there had been. A very little thing. He was just moving in, and there was a box of dishes and stuff on the counter in the kitchen. When I found him I thought he was still alive, so I went in the kitchen to get some water, and I looked in the cabinet there, right near the sink. And what do you think I found?" He paused for a beat. "Two coffee cups. That's all. two coffee cups that had been rinsed and put in the cabinet. They were still damp. I picked one up to fill with water. I didn't notice right away, or didn't think about it, but when I picked the cup up it left a little ring on the wood of the shelf. A little ring. The cup had been dried, but there was just this little ring of condensation from having been wet. I remember noticing that. But I was in a desperate hurry. But later, I remembered that little detail. You know what it meant?"

"That someone else was there—"

"Someone who rinsed out two cups and put them in the cabinet within the last hour or so, at most a couple of hours. It wasn't Ken who did that. There were other dirty glasses and dishes there, in the sink, on the table. It wasn't Ken who put them there."

Dr. Rosenstone

BEFORE HIS WEEKLY with Lyman Wilbur, Dr. Rosenstone felt the need to prepare himself. The writer was, after all, now a sort of colleague of Eloise Kness. And Rosenstone was feeling mightily frustrated by the turn of events.

Furthermore, this was the person to whom the doctor had entrusted his theory of the blame for the death of Ken Preston, a sharing of information which had resulted in exactly nothing. Of course it had since come to light that the prescription pills involved were tranquilizers, not sedatives. Much less likely to fatally overdose. But still, the principle of the reckless prescribing of drugs and Kness's role with Preston remained, and ought to have at least been investigated or made public.

Nothing. She just rolled along on her fat little legs, munching a knish as she went. He washed his hands of her, of all of them.

But then Wilbur's session took a surprising turn back to the death of Kenny Preston. Rosenstone had seen the writer's quickly improving health and confidence. It was on full display this morning.

"My friend downtown hinted they are looking at a person to charge in Preston's death. It's the friend of his, the newspaperman?"

"Joe?" Rosenstone considered a moment. "Well, no. I mean, I understand the thinking, I guess. They think like cops, they want to find bad guys, but I was there that night, along with Joe. He had not committed a murder. Kenny Preston was on a bender. Joe was stone sober. He'd just got there."

"But they haven't talked to you, the police or anybody?"

"Not since that weekend."

Wilbur leaned back, and seemed to be sort of reveling in his downtown cop friend. "The police think this Joe was with him earlier. Somebody was. Preston was at home, and his car was ten miles away. And Joe may have been sober that night, but there had been incidents with the two of them before then. Drunkenness. The two of them were in a brawl at some saloon. There was a report, but no charges."

This was news to Rosenstone. "I'm sorry to hear that. That would be a relapse for Joe. That was who he was when I met him. I thought he had gotten better."

"They are also thinking he was having an affair with her."

The doctor laughed. "With Pamela? When? When would she have the time? Sometimes the male sexual imagination confers amazing powers on women."

Wilbur shrugged. "Perhaps she had spurned him?"

"That I could see. Actually that's what I would expect."

"Perhaps he was angry?"

"Who knows?" Dr. Rosenstone did not see this as anything but idle noodling. He was ready to move on to another topic.

"And they wonder about his article in the *Star,* casting suspicion on Morton Blackwell."

Rosenstone's impatience boiled over. "From what I know of Joe, he may wear his heart on his sleeve, but he's just not devious enough to abet someone's death and then try to shift the blame. If you really want to come up with a theory of the death, look at the drugs involved and the failure of the psychoanalytic treatment. I doubt it's murder, but it's a rotten shame."

CHAPTER FOURTEEN

"Angeline Introduces a Radiant New Face, But Fails to Inspire" (Review, *The Dayton, Ohio News*, December 5, 1947)

JOHAN FELSENER'S BEST-SELLING account of the life of St. Angeline of Umbria is a hymn to the everlasting beauty of innocence and faith. Pamela Carr, in her first film, is given the task of playing the fifteenth-century teenage girl who was first castigated and later canonized for her religious devotion. It is a delicate and exacting role, and Miss Carr pulls it off with a complete sureness of touch.

Angeline is a complex character, virginal but worldly, an heiress to a position and wealth who is orphaned as a child and rejects her elevated social status after experiencing a vision that called her to a religious life. She transforms from a simple and pious soul to an inspired, charismatic recruiter for virginity and repentance. Her unabashed belief in her cause, and forthright pursuit of it, soon leads to conflicts with both ecclesiastical and civil authorities, who seem to feel (though the movie has the good taste never to state it so crudely) that Angeline is some sort of Pied Piper who will depopulate the country of virtuous girls. Before long she stands accused of both sorcery and heresy.

To its credit, the film does not make Angeline's opponents into sanctimonious autocrats. The philosophical arguments are reasoned on all sides, and even the Duke of Milan (James Justice), the biggest of the big cheeses, admits to his fallibility.

And therein lies the problem. The religious arguments

soon lose their impact, and conflicts and resolutions begin to seem contrived. This is somewhat the fault of those who dared to try making an inspirational but discursive book into a feature film. And while Miss Carr's beauty, more radiant than ravishing, can stand up to repeated, lingering views, the story soon loses its dynamic tension. Movies are meant to move, events to happen, characters to act. The fault, I fear, lies not so much in the rather pedestrian direction of Henry Koehler as it does in the tendency of producer Morton Blackwell to overdo themes and underline points. In red pencil. Twice. Though not officially credited as either director or writer, Blackwell's fingerprints are all over this film, in the didactic plot, the overbaked emotions, the constant effort to achieve *spectacle* rather than just tell a story.

The acting is uniformly fine. Brett Walsh, in particular, invests the character of Angeline's priestly defender with a sense of the struggle between the earthly and the celestial in a simple, good-hearted man. And Jane Revere, as Sister . . . .

CHAPTER FIFTEEN
January 1948

Morton

THE ANNOUNCEMENT CAME on January 14th, 1948, that *Angeline* had been nominated for an Academy Award for Best Picture, and Pamela Carr for Best Actress, Leading Role. On the day the news came out, the movie, which had been released November 26, had already earned $3.85 million, or approximately double the cost of the production. This treasure trove cancelled out the overbudget production costs, and the overlong shooting schedule. It was now on pace to become the highest-grossing Blackwell picture yet.

Mort tapped on the door of Mrs. B.'s office, and stuck his head in. She was busy as usual, but when he gave her the news about the nominations she got up and came over to give him a congratulatory hug. Mutually congratulatory, for Mort was well aware of how much she had contributed to Pamela's wonderful performance.

"This one is yours," he said. "If we win. But win or lose, we've already won."

"It's thrilling!" She allowed herself a single exultant laugh. "Let's enjoy this!"

He told her the new B.O. numbers and she giggled. "My goodness, it's so perfect! It really is!"

"This is what it's all about," said Mort. He loved his wife and children, and his parents and his brother. But he really believed—though he would admit it to no one—that success in the movies was the most important thing in life. Real success. He was tasting that now for the first time since 1941, and the flavor was as sweet as he remembered.

"Pamela is a major star," said Mrs. B., leaning on her desk. "That's an accomplished fact. No more *maybe,* no more *she's going to be.* She is. Now."

"You're right, and she's a pony we can ride again and again. Her next one will knock their socks off."

"She deserves it. She was such a trouper, through all the heartbreak."

"Yes, indeed." Mort wanted to call Pamela and tell her, be the first to tell her, but first he had to let Elaine know the good news. But he would not go into the financials. His wife was very aware of the numbers. In fact, Mort was fairly certain that she had a spy in the accounting section. As far as she was concerned, half of all profits were hers, especially since the studio, and Mort and Elaine personally, had drifted so close to financial disaster the last two years.

They would celebrate Saturday night at the Cafe Trocadero, the official movie industry banquet hall. All the producers would be there, all the directors and writers and actors reveling in their own, and each other's, success, while the losers, the also-rans, would look on with barely-hidden envy.

The next couple of days, at home and at the studio, were wrapped in a golden haze. *Fixation,* as the Stowbridge had finally been named, was well underway. With the new cash flow he could finally give serious consideration to Pamela's next project. But Friday evening Elaine lowered the boom on him. Mort came in at midnight, straight from the office. He had not stopped for a drink at one of his spots. He actually had pretty much squashed that habit of yore, because a drink often turned into three, or 3:30.

This more restrained lifestyle did not come from a new sense of responsibility, or respectability. It was more due to the fact that he was now, at the age of forty-seven, unmistakably in love with a woman half his age. He had not been able to get over Pamela, and had in fact become determined to have her, and to deserve her. Just not to marry her. At least not now. He wanted her to be his permanent, exclusive lover. And he wanted to stay married to Elaine. At least until the boys were grown.

This determination had led him to become much more the husband Elaine wanted. He was drinking less, gambling hardly at all. He had dropped fifteen pounds and become much more committed to exercise and a good diet. And in another oddity, he was seeing less and less of the woman he was in love with. Pamela's mother had been joined by her father and sister, and they had moved to a new home in Sherman Oaks. And her father had become her chauffeur, so the sort of casual late-night liaisons he had enjoyed with Pamela in the past were now impossible. Mort actually didn't mind that, as long as he could be certain that she was waiting for him and him alone.

All these efforts, all these improvements, all for naught.

It was unusual that Elaine would wait up for him, more unusual still that she would be sitting on the sofa, leafing through a magazine, a glass of brown liquor on the table next to her.

"Get yourself a drink." She lay the magazine aside. There was a businesslike tone to that sentence that put Mort on notice. He poured it stiff. Straight.

She waited until he had seated himself in the easy chair. She had been crying. "I want a divorce."

Mort thought a moment before replying, "I know."

"You're not surprised?"

"No, not surprised. But I've been afraid of it. We've been drifting apart."

"I'm not drifting," she scoffed. "I'm right here where I've always been. But you just don't give a goddamn about this marriage or me anymore."

Mort tried to meet her anger with understanding. "That's not true."

"No, it is." She let out a slow, quiet sigh. "Your priorities have shifted. I used to put up with your peccadillos because I knew that I was Number One. I'm not Number One anymore.

"You and the kids—"

"Let's get past that, shall we? I'm already past it. Well past. In fact Pamela Carr may be the best thing that ever happened to me. Monday morning my lawyers are filing for divorce. My accountant is going to have people going over your books. I suggest you cooperate with them. And we are dissolving our business arrangement. I will be taking half the assets as they existed at close of business today. And half the income from now until, well . . . that can be worked out."

Much as he had wanted to avoid this conversation, Mort was ready for it. "I'm not going to fight you over that. I want the boys and you to be taken care of always. But this is not a good time. It's going to put me in a bind."

"No, this is the perfect time." She gave him a sad, sardonic smile. "You're getting ready to go broke again. *Angeline* is a big success, but you're already spending that money in your head. You're building sets and framing shots. Your Stowbridge is overbudget and overdue, and when you start this new Pamela opus magnum, whatever it is, you're going to spend everything you have, and plenty you don't." She took a sip of her drink. "It's now or never for me. I am so sad that it has come to this." Tears rimmed her eyes. "But it has. It definitely has."

Mort got out of his chair and kneeled in front of her. "Look, we can fix this. I know I've been distracted. I know my failings with you, but—"

"Please get up." She patted the sofa next to her, and he sat as instructed.

"Morton, I don't blame you. She's beautiful. And charming. And and you fell in love with her. I have decided I am not going to fight that. But you can't have her *and* me *and* all the money *and* the playhouse. The greatest thing about you is your passion. your commitment. You want to do everything, have everything, know everything, fix everything. But that's also your weakness, because it's impossible to do everything yourself, to control the whole universe." She smiled. "So this is going to be better for you, for me, for her, for the studio."

Mort felt a powerful wave of regret. The things that had first attracted him to Elaine he still felt strongly: her intellect, her honesty, her creativity and clarity. All these were on display at this moment. He had even discussed the possibility of his divorce with Mrs. Brown, who had advised him against it, mainly because of his two children, who were at a crucial age: Brian in his first year of prep school, and Gordon just two years behind him. Just the time when children would have the most difficulty adjusting to the destruction of their family.

But Mort had known this was coming, and he had come up with a plan. "I have a proposal for you."

She snorted. "Is that a joke?"

"Very definitely not." Mort stood up, walked back to the bar, and picked up his glass. "Elaine Blackwell Productions. You take the same assets. You form a completely separate business entity, incorporated, so protected from anything I do. I will support our household, all the expenses, but I will have no say in your company, and no interest. You get rich, you get rich. You go broke, you go broke. And the same for me and the studio. All of that will be legally and financially separated from our marriage."

He took a deep breath. "And we stay married."

Elaine stared into her scotch. She seemed about to speak, but something held her. At that moment Mort felt a deep, throbbing chord of emotion, a memory and an appreciation of all they had been to each other.

Finally she spoke. "That's sort of, what they might call a French Proposal, wouldn't you agree?"

He shrugged.

"Well, darling, you surprise me again." She stood up and walked over to look out the big glass door for a long moment. Then she turned and headed out of the room. Over her shoulder she said, "I'll sleep on it. Don't forget to turn out the lights, will you?"

Pamela

THE STUDIO, THAT is say, Morton Blackwell, had invited a group of about twenty to celebrate the Best Picture, Best Actress, and Best Costume nominations for *Angeline* on Saturday evening. This was to be at a nightclub that Priscilla had never been to, though she'd certainly heard of it. The whole group, less one, now sat in limousines in the parking lot of the Blackwell Studios executive offices.

Priscilla was in the second of the four cars with her mother Jessie, Mrs. Brown, and Brett Walsh and his wife. Brett was the male lead from *Angeline*. He was more of a rugged character actor than a leading-man type—*Angeline,* being a religious and inspirational movie didn't have a romantic aspect. But there had been talk at the studio that he might "snag" a "nom" for his role as the priest who was Angeline's spiritual guide. That had not happened, though if Brett was disappointed, he hid it effectively. He had been in the army during the war, in the Italian campaign. He wasn't going to cry about an acting award.

They were waiting for Morton, who was still in the office. Priscilla assumed he would be riding in the first car with his wife Elaine and the director, Henry, and his wife. Priscilla's relationship with Mort still did not officially exist, though everyone knew about it, she felt sure. Except maybe Mort's wife. What everyone did not know was that the relationship had ceased to be a sexual one, though it was still romantic and affectionate.

The drivers had turned off the car engines, as everyone seemed to share the unspoken knowledge that waiting for Mort Blackwell came with no time limit. Priscilla, however, was impatient to get going. She was coming to realize that impatience had always been part of her character, a part which she had become so practiced at hiding that no one ever seemed to realize it existed. Both the impatience and the suppression of it were inheritances from her mother. She was seeing these things now that they were living together for the fist time in years. And the first time in Priscilla's adulthood.

Doc Rosenstone considered this particular kind of emotional self-control in Priscilla to be a neurotic, hostile impulse that would be expressed in other ways. But he had also taught her tricks for dealing with her impatience. She took a long, slow, deep breath. Six counts in, eight counts out. As she visualized the oxygen flowing in and out, she made a conscious decision of acceptance. When it's the boss you are waiting for, not to mention your host for the evening, what do you do?

You wait. You make conversation. Finally Mort strolled out the door, looking quite resplendent in a dinner jacket. As they watched him stroll up to the first car, Brett Walsh said, "What the hell? Nobody told me this was black tie."

"It's not." Mrs. B. touched Brett's wife on the knee. "We're not getting all gowned for this dinner. He just likes to show off."

"You look fine," said Jessie.

"Yeah," said Mrs. Walsh. "He's probably going to get on stage with Cugat."

All four women laughed. Brett smiled uncertainly. And though she joined in the laughter, Priscilla had that feeling again that everyone in the room was in on the joke but her. They had all been in the town longer than her, knew more people, heard more stories, nodded more knowingly.

But at least the caravan was now underway. Mama sat in the middle of the back seat, with Priscilla on one side and Mrs. Walsh on the other. Mrs. B. and Brett sat on the jump seat facing them.

Now that they were moving, Priscilla found herself in a

pensive mood, excited but also anxious about the new level of fame and scrutiny she was entering. The publicity for *Angeline* had been unusual. Because of the nature of the role, Pamela Carr's background had been largely hidden, while the few tidbits of her story that were put out emphasized her youth and innocence, and her status as a Hollywood newcomer.

"Because the public knows," the PR man had told her, "that Hollywood corrupts, and Hollywood stardom corrupts absolutely." He looked very pleased with the line, but Priscilla felt he'd used it before.

As they drove, her mother, sensing her mood, leaned close and whispered, "He'd be very proud."

Priscilla shook her head. "Don't say that."

"I'm going to say it. Somebody should."

"Oh, Mama."

"He was very proud of you. As an actor and as a person. We all are."

"But that was Priscilla Preston! Don't you see? She's as dead as he is!"

Her mother glanced at her in disbelief, or disgust, then emitted a rheumy chuckle. "Life isn't that simple, dear."

Priscilla did not reply. The pain of Kenny's loss had never been sharper, but she was now, tonight, entering a world where that pain would be plastered over by the *image* of the pain, by how she was *seen as* reacting to, or living with, the pain. She had loved creating the part of Angeline for six months. But she had slowly realized that another character was also being created. Pamela Carr. Angeline was complete now, safely on the screen. Pamela would be with her for life, every time she turned a corner, every day she woke, every night she went to sleep. And part of Pamela would always be the headstrong, ambitious yet foolish and self-centered girl who had betrayed her husband, who in his turn became so forlorn at her heartlessness that he killed himself. "It's going to come out. I'm going to have to deal with it. I will never be able to think of this movie without thinking of Kenny. And other people are going to think the same thing."

"It was an accident," said Jessie.

"They've been protecting me."

Jessie patted her hand. "As well they should."

"But they can't protect me anymore."

Kenny's death was not a secret. Up to now, it also was not talked about. But sooner or later someone was going to ask, to bring it up. Someone other than the *Star*, the scandal sheet that everyone pretended they didn't read. Even they hadn't written anything since right after the accident. Priscilla wondered if that was because Mort had clamped down on them somehow. Or was it because *that* was something that happened to unknown actress Priscilla Preston, who had since faded into obscurity. Now it would be something else entirely.

Mrs. Brown said, "You should enjoy this. You may not understand how precious it is."

Priscilla was looking out the window, purposely avoiding looking at her mother or anyone else in the car. "But people are going to ask, *Why did you leave him? Why were you having an affair?* That's what killed him. He never hurt me. I hurt him."

Jessie leaned closer to her ear. "You couldn't control him. You can't put the weight of his death on your shoulders. He made his choices."

Priscilla saw movement and glanced at Mrs. B., who was also leaning toward her. She glimpsed Brett looking at her from the far corner of the compartment. For a split second she wondered what he must think of her.

"He wasn't just self-destructive," said Mrs. B. "He wasn't acting out of love. It was spite. He thought if he could wreck your career he could get you back, and you could go back to New York and be poor but happy again. Or something like that. That was bad for you, but it also could have been a disaster for the studio. There was a major investor who was already threatening to pull out because of the problems we were having. One more thing, and he would have done it."

"But that was after Ken . . ."

"No, actually, he never even heard about that. He's in New York. This was right before Ken . . ."

Priscilla breathed a shaky sigh.

Jessie said, "Okay, let's change the subject. Mr. Walsh, how did you like making this movie?"

"I liked it fine. It was a thrill, really. Working with Priscilla—Pamela—was great. She really knows her stuff. But she told me you were an actress, too? And an impresario—"

Priscilla could no longer contain herself. "I miss him! He was my first love, and the only man who ever made me feel complete!"

There was silence in the car. She had shocked them, Priscilla realized without regret. She was back in her night at the beach, trying to end it all. She felt again the crushing weight of Ken's sad and lonely death. Compared to that, what she had had to go through had been little enough, but now it overwhelmed her. She had been a good girl, had put on a happy face, shoulder to the wheel, nose to the grindstone, and everyone had said how strong she was, how noble. Inside she was crumbling and withering like rotten fruit.

Jessie hugged her. Mrs. B. looked out the window. Brett reached out and touched her arm. Her perfumed, successful, living arm.

"It's okay kid," he said. "Everything's gonna be alright."

Anna

IN EARLY 1944, before things began to come completely undone in Berlin, when there were still stores and theaters and streetcars, Anna was in a play in a rickety old music hall in Tauentzienstrasse. Actually, to call it a play was very kind. It was really just a review, but focused on drama, on the classics. Of course classics, because anything modern or even hinting at avant-garde was certain to be shut down by the RKK, the culture ministry. And there was no money for new settings and costumes, so the actors would rummage through trunks of old hats, vests, masks and scarves, then go on stage and do monologues, readings, short scenes of Hauptman and Schiller. The stark settings, the harsh light of a single arc lamp in a darkened room, seemed to Anna to increase the dramatic intensity and to match the ever-present fear and sorrow the audience brought with them into the theater. Usually air-raid sirens would go off before the second act, and everyone would file out of the theatre into the bomb shelters.

During the days Anna's UFA art department was pressed into service painting numbers and index lines on aircraft instrument dials. One day, as she was getting ready to leave there, the directress, Timken, stopped her.

"Hoelscher needs to rehearse a scene tonight. You have to stay. We need to get this done."

This request caught Anna in a dilemma. Hoelscher's new film was one of the few worthwhile projects to be found at the state film studio. "But I'm due at the theater at seven thirty, at the latest."

"No." Timken shook her head obstinately. "We will not be done by then."

Did she not understand? "But that's a *job*. At least they give me a meal, and money sometimes, if it's a good night."

Timken grabbed Anna's arm and looked up at her with a sort of pleading that was rare for the directress, usually so peremptory. "But this could be your break in films. Karolyn can't come. She's ill. And we need someone. These are desperate times, and this could be an important film for public morale."

Anna laughed. "For *public morale?* When did you become an air-raid warden?"

"Well it could," sniffed Timken. "But more important, it's good work. You know it. You know Gerd."

Anna did know that. And she did know Gerd Hoelscher, a brilliant and principled artist. So she went back into the empty warehouse that was now the soundstage, and they rehearsed with a few other actors. It seemed to be a reworking of *The Mayor of Zalamea,* but with improvised staging and dialogue. Anna was lost as to how this old-fashioned drama would inspire anyone to push the English and the Americans back into the sea. But she already knew well enough that what happens before the camera is only a sort of pantomime, not to be understood by the actors until days or weeks or months later, after editing and retakes and dubbing and all the rest. As the filming is taking place, the finished movie exists in the mind of the director and nowhere else.

They worked almost until midnight, when it was far too late to go to the theater. Anna slept on a couch in the office that night, having gone without dinner.

There was no more rehearsal of the all-important film, and no mention of it by Timken or anyone else. So a few days later Anna asked her, "What happened to Gerd's film?"

The directress looked at her in alarm. They were in the hallway, with people coming and going. "Cancelled!"

She hurried down the hall. When Anna walked by the open door of her office a few minutes later, Timken waved her in, and motioned to shut the door. When Anna turned back into the room, Timken was tiptoeing up to her with a strained expression that seemed quite comical. Anna almost chuckled, but strange behavior or not, Frau Timken was a person of authority who deserved her respect.

She took Anna by the arm. "Goebbels called that afternoon," she whispered. "He invited you to dinner."

Anna was sure she'd misheard. "What? I'm sorry. Who?"

"Yes. Him." Timken stared at her without wavering. "Him. I told him you couldn't come, due to work on the picture. He could hardly argue, since the film has been prioritized by the Propaganda Ministry."

Anna still wasn't sure what she was hearing. "I don't believe this. How does he know me from anything?"

"He may have seen you at the theater."

Now Anna understood. A shiver of revulsion grabbed her by the spine. She slid down into the chair by the desk. "God! He might have!"

"So we couldn't let you go there. I talked to Gerd. And of course we had to do real work, because it might have got back to him. There are many rats in this building who might scurry around to the Party looking for, well, whatever they look for."

This risk that Timken took, lying to Goebbels and then staging the scene to prove the lie, was still, to Anna, four years later, one of the bravest and finest things she had ever witnessed. What that dinner might have led to Anna could not even now let herself imagine. Now, everyone knew the Nazi leaders were depraved monsters. Now, the newsreel Goebbels, of the thin, dark, creased *Totenkopf*, could be seen for who he was. But during the war, in the streets and rooms of the besieged German capital, those men held the power of salvation and damnation, not to be denied, certainly not to be tricked or trifled with. And yet that was exactly what Timken and Hoelscher, with everything to lose, that was what they had done to protect her.

ANNA HAD NOT been invited back to tea since her first visit, though she had seen Marlene once more at some gathering of the informal Germanic émigré group, and the star had greeted her warmly, inquired as to her husband and family and career. Marlene herself felt her film career had somewhat stalled, and she was focused on developing her singing, so when Anna heard from her again, it was an invitation to the Trocadero, where she was going to be "doing a couple of numbers" with the Xavier Cugat orchestra.

As she and Ferdie walked up to the door of what looked like a hunting lodge, Anna expected a rather quiet evening in a half-filled dance hall. But around a corner from the foyer there opened up in front of her a large, noisy room with a high, shiny ceiling and people, lots of people, all of them talking and laughing, turning around, getting up, leaning across tables, ordering from waiters. Anna stopped, uncertain.

Ferdie, at her elbow, leaned in. "There she is."

Following his eyes Anna saw, at the back of the room, a booth that seemed to contain a dozen people, but shimmering among them was a silvery image, almost motionless. That was Marlene, listening, smiling, almost seeming to be floating there like a genie, liable to vanish at any second.

As she and Ferdie approached the table, Anna recognized Abby, Louise, the redhead, Joyce, and two other women from the tea. There were other women and three men at the table, and Marlene was busy rearranging several plates of food and passing them back to their owners. Room was made, introductions exchanged, and the conversation continued with barely a ripple. The orchestra at the other end of the room was playing some kind of rhumba music, and it was very good, but it quieted the crowd only slightly during the tunes. In between numbers, people from a group near the bandstand would rise and speak into the microphone. Anna followed very little of what they said. Soon she was passed a plate which contained mussels with a sauce, a poached egg on asparagus with another sauce, and a couple of ribs, possibly lamb, all artfully arranged by Marlene.

Anna looked out at the crowd. She was reminded of the scene in the cartoon film *Pinocchio* of the boys turning into braying donkeys. She had not watched this movie until recently, because of course all American movies were banned in Germany during the war. In the film, the kidnapped children lose all sense of manners and decency and become pathetic, selfish animals fighting and bullying each other to get the things they want. Anna saw something like that here, in the loud voices, the extravagant behavior, the gaudy clothes. She could almost hear the braying. And this was the herd she was striving to become part of. She glanced at Ferdie, and he was not seeing what she was seeing. He was starstruck and impressed.

When everyone was eating, and their glasses were full, Marlene looked around the table with quiet satisfaction. Then she stood up and headed toward the stage. When the people in the crowd saw her, there was spontaneous applause, the first time the room had been focused on anything since Anna arrived. After consulting with the bandleader for a moment, she sang "Falling in Love Again," This was followed by "Lili Marleen" with verses in English, German and French. the end of which Anna was reminded of the phrase about the audience eating out of the performer's hand. Anna had a change of heart. The people in the crowd were not the braying asses of Pinocchio but simply people like her, no better, no worse. They might wear silly and inappropriate dresses that utterly failed to impress, they might say ignorant things, eat unhealthy food, drink too much, have children they could not properly take care of. But when they sat in a crowd and listened to a woman singing a sad, beautiful song they were entranced and transported, just as Anna was.

> Give me a rose to show how much you care,
> Tie to the stem a lock of golden hair.
> Surely tomorrow, you'll feel blue
> But then will come a love that's new . . .

> *Wenn sich die spaeten Nebel dreh'n*
> *Werd' ich bei der Laterne steh'n*
> *Wie einst, Lili Maerleen . . .*

A song about two people in a war, their hope to survive, and a human faith that must endure even when hope is lost. They were just people, like her.

When Marlene returned to the table, the men had disappeared. A few of the women murmured praise, which Marlene acted as if she had not heard. She said, "I saw someone sitting up there. An old friend."

She did not continue. Someone said, "Who was it?"

Marlene broke into a pixielike smile. "I won't tell you. You have to guess. Ten questions. You have to guess from the clues."

The women chuckled and drew in closer.

"They have to be yes or no questions," said Marlene. "Joanna, you start."

Joanna, the sharp-looking brunette, said, "Is he older than you?"

Marlene shook her head and raised an index finger.

A very young but rather mousy blonde asked, "Is he taller than Tyrone Power?"

Shake. "Two."

Joanna: "Is he a disgusting toad with slimy skin?"

Marlene smiled and nodded, holding up three fingers.

Jane, the redhead: "Is he hung like a mouse?"

Nod. "Four."

Louise: "Probably a homo?"

"Five!" Marlene laughed. "A few hints. Is he the worst lay in Hollywood? Would he bang Shirley Temple or Ma Kettle? Yes and yes."

Carol said, "Has he been on stage tonight?"

Marlene laughed and nodded.

Carol continued. "Well we know it wasn't Betty Hutton. And probably not Huston. So it's either Cugat or—"

Marlene raised her hand like a conductor and they all said it together. *"Mort Blackwell!"*

Anna shivered in amazement, then howled with glee. She hugged the girls next to her. Some people up near the stage noticed a ruckus in the back of the room and turned to see what was going on.

One of them may have been Morton Blackwell in a brand-new dinner jacket.

Pamela

BEING AT THE nightclub on this evening unleashed a storm of emotions in Priscilla. That's what it felt like: a violent storm, a heavy rain after a drought, both scary and a great relief, a feeling that if we can just get through the next couple of hours, things will be much better. Faces were stepping off the movie screens of yesterday and today to lean close to her, smile, shake hands, congratulate. It was disorienting to think that *she*, Pamela Carr, had the Academy Award nomination—not Greer Garson, not Joan Fontaine, not David Niven or Carl Blanchard, or God help us, Helen Hayes—all of whom floated by.

And Mort was getting even more attention. They came from all over the room and in such numbers that for awhile, Mort and Elaine stood up to create a kind of receiving line. And Mort was in his element—the man who knows everyone, smiling and introducing Pamela, who felt lame and awkward. She had nothing to say, so she introduced her mother, who acted like a member of the school board on parent-teacher night.

Through this onslaught Priscilla noticed that Mrs. B. was hardly mentioned or noticed, and was introduced to or shook hands with only the few people she seemed to know. Priscilla thought this unfair and unjust. Didn't anyone understand how important Mrs. B. was? After nearly a year at the studio, Priscilla certainly did. Not to mention the personal attention Priscilla had received from her.

But Priscilla also understood the personalities involved. This wasn't anyone's night but Morton Blackwell's. He defined himself by success, and this movie was a success. And since Pamela Carr was his creation, her performance was also his success. And Priscilla understood that tonight was his chance to show her off as his lover, his mistress, an exquisite peach-faced lovebird on his shoulder. In the bizarre, real-unreal world of the theatre and movies, footlights-backstage-curtain up-curtain call, to show her off while standing next to his wife, also beautiful, smart and successful. Most of the people he spoke to probably believed that Pamela was Mort's lover, and that he could show her off in front of his wife and show his wife off in front of his lover, and no one could do anything but admire his harem. And he could do this because he was Morton Blackwell, the greatest producer and greatest lover of them all.

And Mrs. Brown seemed quite content to be ignored, gazing up at Mort and Elaine with genuine delight.

Once the admiring wave had passed and the communicants wandered off to other missions, Priscilla was surprised to see Doc Robbie approaching her. She was even more surprised that he did not seem to recognize her as made his way around the table and slid into a chair next to Elaine, who chirped with joy and quickly enfolded him in a mothering embrace. Mort also smiled and clapped a hand on his shoulder.

Priscilla turned to her other side, where Mrs. B. was also watching the scene with approval. She leaned toward Priscilla. "He came in on *Fixation*. He replaced the, you know, the Jewish mother."

Priscilla understood that Mrs. B was talking about Mort's latest, the psychodrama directed by Stowbridge that had, she'd heard, become a psychodrama itself.

She had not heard this from Mort. Given the routine that had developed since her mother moved in with her, and then her father, the time she could spend with Mort was now quite limited. When she lived in the hotel while working on *Angeline*, Mort would visit her almost every night, telling her his work problems endlessly and obsessively. Now he seemed to hoard every moment with her, and to dote on her like the dull, lifeless suitor her mother insisted he be.

But still a married suitor. He had assured both Priscilla and Jessie that his divorce would already be underway if not for complicated tax and financial issues. Surprisingly, Jessie appeared to accept this excuse more readily than Priscilla did.

Priscilla was still visiting Doc Robbie weekly for both personal and group sessions. She of course knew that Elaine Blackwell was also one of his patients—that connection, through Mrs. B., was how Priscilla got the referral. But she had never seen Elaine at Doc Rosenstone's clinic, or heard him talk about her in any but the most passing way.

She had no time to linger over these thoughts because Mrs. B. suddenly rose, or was scooped up, into the arms of Dolores Clark, whose shining eyes and brilliant smile seemed as overpowering at that moment as they would in a perfectly lit and photographed close-up. Mrs. B.'s smile was just as warm, and the two stood embracing, laughing and chatting so affectionately that Priscilla realized how silly it was to worry about Mrs. B. being ignored.

Dolores must have seen Priscilla's wondering look because she hugged Mrs. B. again and said, "This wonderful person helped me adopt my darling daughter!"

When the movie star had departed, and the evening had moved on a little, Priscilla said, "Dolores Clark is so beautiful!"

"Yes." Mrs. B. smiled.

"And she's sure fond of you."

Mrs. B. regarded her thoughtfully. Priscilla thought there was a secret on the older woman's tongue that was about to come out. There was, but it couldn't come out at this table.

"Y'know," said Mrs. B. "I think I'll go powder my nose. Want to?" She gave Priscilla that slightly obtuse angle of a look well-known to women in Hollywood, South Dakota, and probably Nova Scotia, too.

"Yes," said Priscilla. "*Moi aussi.*"

As they slowly waded through the noisy crowd toward the bathroom, Mrs. B. told Priscilla the story in whispered snatches. "It was six years ago, when Dolores was a rising star at . . . I forget which studio. She got knocked up by—" Mrs. B. looked around, and shrugged. "A married actor, let's say. It couldn't be allowed for her career, or for his. But she's Catholic, and she wouldn't take care of it. You know. So instead she took a vacation to Europe and had the baby, and, well, the little girl ended up with me. There was a connection she called upon. Greggy was only three months older and I was just in the steno pool then. And Steve was still alive. So I had more time and it meant a little money, and it was just easy. Cindy is a darling little girl."

Priscilla didn't know whether to be horrified or impressed. "My god, the level of the BS!"

They were outside the restroom now. "You don't know," said Mr. B., leaning closer. "So I had the baby for over a year. Dolores would come by when she could, but it had to be in secret. And she didn't have much free time anyway. Then one day I took Cindy to Maryvale, the orphanage, and the next day Dolores adopted her." Mrs. B. laughed. "*Then* it was in the papers."

Priscilla was stunned. "You're miraculous! Truly. You can make people disappear and appear."

Mrs. B. put a finger to her lips and disappeared herself, into the restroom. In that moment it came to Priscilla, and she stood there where she was, not seeing anything. Not hearing the music.

CHAPTER SIXTEEN
Soon After

Lyman

"LYMAN WILBUR SAT in the giant, fake-cowhide chair facing the giant stone fireplace. The huge fire there blazed so fiercely that it made the big, high-ceilinged ski lodge uncomfortably warm. The wall of floor-to-ceiling windows at the other side of the room looked out on deep snow, fir trees and the slopes of a Utah ski resort, the whole scene lit by a brightly shining sun."

Lyman reread the awkward sentences to grade them. Descriptively accurate? Narratively dynamic? It was just an academic exercise, after all. He looked around at the scene again. The mountains, the lodge, the fireplace, and the chair had clearly been designed for a race of immense Nordic warriors, but the only people he saw in the room on this weekday morning were the gaffers, the gofers, the grips and electricians and technicians of a film crew. Most of them were wearing some version of ski clothes, while Lyman had on his usual Krappenheimer suit. The crew was waiting to film location scenes Morton Blackwell had insisted on for *Fixation*. They were waiting because the sun this morning was so overpoweringly bright and cast such strong shadows that they could not get the scenes the director, Stowbridge, wanted.

So they waited and watched to see if the bank of clouds that currently hid the peak of the mountain might migrate downslope and block or at least filter the light. And Lyman was writing about his surroundings out of the boredom of waiting in a place where one must stay with nothing constructive to do. He had completed his new pages for the script the previous night and this morning. But Stowbridge had not seen the rewrite yet, and he might ask for changes or something completely different. The director had not seen the pages because he had been preoccupied with the sun, the shadows, the angles, the glare off the snow, and the color of the lead actress's makeup.

Lyman had a manuscript in progress up in his room for a new Archer Daniels book. That was what he wanted to be doing, driving his tough-but-tender hero through the dark streets of the Long Beach waterfront looking for the one-eyed bank robber Cortez Kelly.

But he could not do that. He looked at his notepad and reread the description he had just written. He had used *giant* twice. He changed the second one to *great*. The great stone fireplace.

Someone had left a *Hollywood Reporter* on the lacquered log table next to his chair. Lyman picked it up and idly leafed through it. He soon came upon a spread of photos and typically breathless blurbs of recent Hollywood events, premieres, fund-raisers, parties. And there, top center left, sitting behind a tablecloth and glasses of water, sat Mort Blackwell and his wife, along with Pamela Carr—Priscilla—and to her right, partially cropped out, Blackwell's assistant Mrs. Brown.

A year ago these people were strangers to him. Now the man in the picture with the glasses and wavy hair was paying his salary and red-lining his writing. Screen writing that is. Lyman had long since learned to differentiate that from his real writing, the kind that paid pennies on the page. In the photo Mort's mouth was half open and slightly askew. He was talking. Of course. Pamela, in the center of the picture, was listening. She could not take a bad picture. Her facial structure and expression somehow suggested both tantalizing mystery and a sort of willful innocence.

These were people in his life now.

A year ago he'd stood over Tina's grave knowing he could not return to hear the unending silence of the house they shared and the life for which she had been the only real purpose. Since that time he had fought the bottle to a draw, his career had improved, he had found a way to carry on until he could come up with a reason to keep living without her. But he had not yet come up with that reason. He was a clock that had been wound for the last time and would keep ticking, keep moving, until it stopped. Does a clock know when it will stop? Can it feel the unwinding of the spring, sense the declining tension in the gears? Lyman thought not. The clock moves until it stops, surprised at its own silence.

Silence. The lack of anyone he cared about saying anything that mattered followed him around now like a hungry dog. The most heartbreaking thing was that even in his memory, Tina had stopped speaking to him. He could picture her face, dream of her smile, but she never spoke to him. He could remember conversations they had had, sometimes gay, sometimes heartbreaking, sometimes routine. But his memory never delivered her voice, her sentences, her tone, so important in knowing the meaning. He did not need for her to say anything in particular, just to speak.

Boredom had become a powerful force in his life. When he took his walks on the beach he made sure to keep his mind busy. Thinking about the story he was writing, or how to fix the world, or about the people in his past, the places, the times, the turning points. But that was his own time. The rest of the day was usually filled with repetitious, unrewarding chores whose only value was that they kept him from even more repetitious, even less rewarding chores.

Mort had not come with the crew up to Utah, probably because that might have pushed Stowbridge over the line into committing a murder instead of just filming one. But the memos kept coming, via early morning telegrams and sometimes by courier, and Lyman received his share. The change from Dr. Kness to Dr. Rosenstone had meant a rewriting of the psychological . . . mumbo jumbo, as far as Lyman was concerned, and he knew Stowbridge generally agreed with him.

But the rewrites were keeping Lyman on the payroll, and had brought him to Utah, a big country with big chairs and big fireplaces. This was not a fire such as the one Kenny Preston had started to burn his furniture. This conflagration would consume an entire bedroom set without burping. Who was it who had told Lyman about Kenny burning his furniture, about the sad, smoldering seat cushions or whatever they were? Must have been Doc R. He was there that night, along with the reporter, Les Joseph, aka Joe. Or maybe he'd read it in that story in the *Star*.

Lyman studied the newspaper photo. Mort was gazing at Pamela. Pamela looking back at Mort, the wife looking at the camera. The other woman, Brown, seen in profile, smiled across the table at the group. Priscilla had told Lyman that Brown was more than an assistant. She had called her a fairy godmother or something. The good witch of the North. Or was she the Wicked One, in the West? She was on the west side of this photo, and her profile somewhat resembled Margaret Hamilton.

Something tickled his memory. That day he had visited Mort's office, he'd met Stowbridge and Mrs. Brown and the first psychiatrist, Dr. Kness. End tables, Mrs. Brown had said when they were talking about Kenny Preston. He burned his bridges and his end tables. What did that mean?

Lyman wondered for a moment what was drawing him back to the sad but unremarkable case of young Mr. Preston. Albie the publicity man came walking by, hands in his pockets. He looked at Lyman. "Bored?"

"Sure. We're all bored. We came to Utah for that very reason." Lyman had a thought. He held up the *Reporter* open to the page with the picture of Mort and the group. "Your people are in the paper."

Albie looked at the picture. "I wish I was there. But someone had to be up here to coordinate things. The resort gave us a deal. Free rooms, free meals. But we have to have our stars frolic in the snow for the cameras. But."

"Conditions were too perfect. I've never heard that before."

"I guess that's one way of looking at it. Perfect for skiing, lousy for filming."

Lyman thought that he was going to move on. Albie was one of those guys who was always on his way to something. But he stopped for a moment. Lyman said, "You remember Kenny Preston?"

Albie gave him a suspicious look. "Sure. A bullet we dodged. Just an accidental overdose. Even with the mystery drug."

"The mystery? What was that?"

"Oh, you know. He had the prescription I guess for the one drug. But they found another one. I forget the name of it, the official name. It's what we used to call a Mickey Finn. You know, back on the docks in New York. The bartender slips the drug in a guy's drink, the guy blacks out, the bartender's friends take him out and take his wallet. Tough times back then, I guess. A lot of stories that never made it in the newspaper."

Now he did wander off. Even so, it was the longest conversation Lyman had ever had with the guy. And he wondered how Albie knew that about the drugs. Had there been some kind of official report, or what? And the Mickey. That was chloral hydrate. Something between an anesthetic and a sleeping potion. Lyman had studied poisons and knockout drops when he was doing his mystery-story apprenticeship writing for *Nightshade,* his first pulp magazine, back in the Depression. Chloral hydrate was a crude drug, never used by doctors but, like Albie said, much abused on some of the meaner streets. It could be dissolved in alcohol, water, tea or coffee. Lyman had once written a short story, never published, about a guy who has some coffee with knockout drops in it. He expects he'll be up all night, but twenty minutes later he's passed out in his car with the motor running when a cop comes up and . . . Lyman forgot the rest. Anyway, a powerful drug.

And Kenny Preston had it in his system? Kenny died of an overdose. The only question had ever been, was it an *accidental* overdose? Lyman had never seriously considered that someone would find Kenny Preston enough of a problem to bump him off. Who would it have been? Mort Blackwell on the jealous lover theory? Joe Giannelli on some other jealous lover theory? Both of those possibilities had been investigated by law enforcement and discarded.

Kenny had shown up at Priscilla's hotel, drunk and belligerent. Getting away from him was how she ended up at Rosenstone's, the morning Lyman met her. And Kenny'd taken a cab home and left his car there at the hotel. That's what Priscilla told him. But it didn't make sense.

And Lyman never thought about it at the time. Now he wondered. Cabs weren't that easy to get in L.A., especially if you were going to the suburbs. That had happened to Lyman his first day out of Doc Rosenstone's hoosegow. The cab company had refused to take him from North Hollywood to Santa Monica. And that was in the middle of the day. They had said, we stay in the city. So somehow a taxi had taken a drunken, angry man from Culver City to Glendale? On a Friday night?

But somehow he got home, leaving his car behind.

Lyman looked again at the picture on his lap. Unlike his dead wife, unlike the unfortunate Kenny Preston, this picture spoke clearly. Ambitions had been realized, traumas soothed, success attained, and the celebration had begun. They won. The picture is a hit. Pamela Carr is famous. The studio is saved.

And Kenny Preston lies in a grave on the outskirts of a small town in Texas.

He never had a chance. The poor sap never had a chance.

Mrs. Brown

THE DOOR TO Carla Brown's office was usually open, because it was just easier. She thought of her job as being "Chief Cook and Bottle Washer," which meant being in charge of nothing, but doing everything. Which meant people walking in and out all the time—secretaries, producers, lawyers, contractors, union reps—everyone involved in the nuts and bolts of running the studio, without appointments She didn't have to say, *my door is always open*, because it always was. Heading off problems and complainers before they could get in front of Mort was a big part of what she did.

She was making notes on the Figby contract when someone said "Excuse me." Looking up she saw Wilbur, the writer on the Stowbridge. tapping the stem of his pipe on the door jamb. "May I interrupt?"

"Yes, certainly. Come in." She had had no contact with this man since the start of the picture, but thought she recalled that he had gone on the location shoot at the ski resort. This might be about that. A problem with the hotel, the travel, or—

"You drove him home."

This was confusing. She immediately thought he was talking about Greggy, but how could he be?

As if answering her question, he said. "Kenny Preston."

She had heard this one was a sort of amateur sleuth. He resembled a pudgy Sherlock Holmes from the movies as he stood before her, one arm across his chest, supporting the elbow of the other arm, which reached up to hold the pipe in front of his face. A rather forced pose of casualness, it seemed to Carla. She said, "I don't understand."

"I had a realization about him the other day,"

"About Kenny Preston? Yes, that was a very sad thing. Was he your friend?"

"Actually I never met him. But I know Miss Carr."

She still wondered where he was headed. "It was a difficult time. I'm so proud of her."

He made a sucking noise on the pipe, which didn't seem to be lit. "And I realized the only way he could have got home that night was for you to drive him."

"By *that night* you mean when he killed himself."

"Yes, you were there."

"Yes, at the hotel. I am the one who suggested Pamela go spend the weekend at Dr. Rosenstone's."

He removed the pipe from his mouth and slid it into his jacket pocket. "That's where I met her, the next morning. She told me she was hiding from her husband, and from her boss. Meaning Blackwell."

"Well, she had to get away from the husband. The rest I wouldn't know about. Kenny was an immediate threat. A danger."

"How was he a threat?"

"He was a danger. And Pri—Pamela wanted him out of there. So I made sure he got home."

"You told her you called a cab. But no cab company would pick up a passed-out drunk and take him anywhere but the hospital."

The cab story had been a convenient thing to tell Pamela. And the police had never asked. She didn't think it was an important point. What did it matter how he got home? What mattered was what happened after he got there, and no one ever asked her about that. But there was no reason to hide it.

"Yes, but because of that, I was able to head off a real tragedy."

"But there *was* a real tragedy."

"You don't understand."

He gave her a superior smile. "Enlighten me."

"Kenny was a desperate man. And he was wildly out of control. We've since learned that he was probably mentally unstable, and his obsession with Pamela was most unhealthy.

"He was in a stupor at that point. I had the address from Pamela, and the bellboy helped me get him into the car and gave me directions. But I got lost anyway and had to stop at a service station. I finally found the place."

"But you didn't just dump him in the front yard."

"No, of course not. He was awake again. He got very angry with me and demanded that I take him back to his car. He was going to go find Pamela. I told him no."

"And he burned his furniture?"

"No, that happened earlier. He told me he had done that." Carla actually welcomed the chance to explain this, to *somebody*. "He went from pathetic to threatening, back and forth, with no warning. But he was almost like someone sleepwalking. He couldn't hold onto a thought for more than about thirty seconds. He had been drinking for hours, and it released all his, inhibitions, I guess. He was just very unstable."

Wilbur removed leaned toward her, his hands on her desk. "But you were in the house?"

"Yes. He went in to call his friend, and I followed him, and tried to calm him down. And it seemed to work, for awhile. I made some coffee, and we sat down there and talked. He told me about how he'd met Pamela, about their time in New York." Carla recalled this conversation with some regret. For just a moment she'd begun to see the likable young man he could be. "But then he suddenly got angry again, and said he was going to get her back. He went into the living room and I saw him get out an overcoat. Then he pulled a gun out of the valise there, and put it in the pocket of the coat. I was frightened about what might happen. He came back in the kitchen and poured some whisky in a glass. When he went to the bathroom, I got the gun out of the coat and left."

"But that's not all you did, is it?"

She didn't care for his tone. "What do you mean?"

"You gave him something. Something to calm him down."

"Yes, relaxing drops."

"Relaxing?" His eyebrows popped up.

"Yes, as you said. Something to calm him. I usually put them in tea, but there was no tea, and I didn't think he would drink any more coffee, since he already poured the whisky. So I put them in the whisky while he was in the bathroom."

"Don't you know they're dangerous?"

Carla felt relieved. Is that what was bothering him? "Oh no. I take them myself. They help me sleep."

He stood up straight, and leaned back a little, as if surprised. "But you can't mix them with alcohol. They're deadly. That's what—"

"Oh no," Carla assured him. "No they're not, I'm sure."

"But you don't drink." He seemed offended.

"Never."

"So you don't know. Where do you get them?"

"From my Chinese doctor."

"Chinese doctor?" His voice rose in seeming disbelief.

"He's not really a doctor. I mean, not an M.D." She wondered if it was worth trying to explain. "Unfortunately in America we have no understanding of ancient wisdom about the body and mind. But I have a whole cabinet full of teas and herbs. I can tell you they work."

"And you have relaxing drops that you put in your tea."

"Yes."

"And they help you sleep."

"It's best with the tea. Passion flower. I give it to my son when he's—"

"You give this stuff to a child?"

"Yes, when he's agitated. It helps him wonderfully. So you can see how safe the drops are."

Morton

THE SUN ROSE over the Los Angeles Basin as an indistinct area of brightness in the sky, obscured by the morning haze. That haze would almost certainly burn off by midday, leaving behind a pleasant afternoon cooled by breezes off the Pacific.

Under this sky, within the complex of large buildings that make up a movie studio, behind a small, manicured lawn, sun shining through a window, Morton Blackwell sat behind his desk, telephone receiver in hand. He glanced at the memo pad at his elbow. The next call would be difficult. It was about money. When he talked to people about work, about the art and craft and business of movies and theatre, he was almost always the one in charge of the conversation, the decision maker. When he talked to certain people about money he was always the debtor, the deadbeat, the profligate.

But he needed another month for *Fixation.* He needed to move ahead with Pamela Carr's new project, *Forever Amber,* or lose the film rights. This was the perfect film for her, and he had to keep it in studio, use his own people, or it just wouldn't fly. And he wanted to keep her happy without marrying her. A great film role would do that.

And he needed money for Brooks. He had many ambitions in life, and one of them was to never again get kicked in the ribs and robbed. Another one was never again to have scandalous and incriminating stories about him printed in the *Star,* or anywhere else that had been planted by one of Brooks's connections.

He had just sold *Angeline* for European distribution, but most of that income would take months to start rolling in, if not years. Half the studio assets were now basically in escrow for the startup of Elaine Blackwell Productions. The money guy, Sullivan, had warned him he was stretching too thin. He would not be happy to get this call. He would threaten Mort with default. He would ask for collateral. Mort would have to shift things around to cover his ass.

The intercom lit up. He pressed the button. Mrs. B. said, "Got a minute?"

"Sure." A brief reprieve. He set the phone back in its cradle.

She came in through the door from her office, carrying her notepad. "This'll just be a minute. It's about the visa extensions for the foreign actors. DiPrizio, Mesnard, Gray, Danley, and a few others. And Marte, of course. She's getting her citizenship this summer. So this'll be the last one for her. You just need to sign this form." Mrs. B. handed him a paper.

Mort scanned the names, wondering whether all these people were needed. But foreign actors' salaries were a pittance. He signed the form.

"And the German? Anna?"

"We opted out. I think she went back there."

"Never could find the right thing for her," said Mort. "Just a little too, master-racey looking. Once again, The Jews That Control Hollywood . . ."

"Yes, you're awful. See you at temple." She chuckled and turned to walk out. "Oh. That new actress, Jeanne Jasper, you wanted to interview. . .do you have time today?"

Mort considered his schedule. "Not until later."

"Ten o'clock look okay?"

"Sure. And that name has to go."

Mrs. B. made a note on her pad.

Someone appeared in the open door behind her. Mort's first reaction was a flash of anger. No one had access through there except . . . Then he recognized the detective from the Kenny Preston thing. And walking in with him a uniformed male cop and some kind of woman cop in a pale blue uniform.

The detective said. "Mrs. Carla Brown?"

ABOUT THIS BOOK

This is a work of fiction by Fred Andersen. It is drawn from stories told by others, in much the same way that historical movies are drawn from research into the history, geography, culture and style of the times and places they are set in. For more on how Hollywood research departments achieved what is known as *verisimilitude* in movies, see my article, "The Warner Bros. Research Department: Putting History to Work in the Classic Studio Era" (*The Public Historian*, 1995). To learn more about some of the history that inspired *Pamela Carr*, see *Star-Crossed: The Story of Robert Walker and Jennifer Jones*, by Beverly Linet, *Showman: the Life of David O. Selznick* by David Thomson, and *The Gift Horse: Report on a Life*, by Hildegard Knef.

IF YOU ENJOYED THIS BOOK

Fred Andersen's previous Hollywood murder mystery, *Lily Torrence* (2014) features more bad behavior by morally questionable Hollywood and Southern California citizens. Available in paper or ebook from your favorite online bookseller.

Visit fxandersen.com for more info, or write to us at palavrpubl@gmail.com.

www.ingramcontent.com/pod-product-compliance
Lightning Source LLC
Chambersburg PA
CBHW070610130626
46556CB00001B/323